KEEP IN TOUCH

Rebecca Chase

Copyright

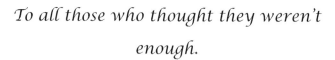

To all those who thought they weren't enough.

Playlist

Firework – Katy Perry

Champagne Supernova – Oasis

High and Dry – Radiohead

Never Had A Dream Come True – S Club 7

Umbrella – Rihanna

C'est La Vie – B*Witched

Wake Me Up When September Ends – Green Day

You Can't Hurry Love – The Supremes

Everywhere – Fleetwood Mac

Black and White Town – Doves

Save Your Tears – The Weeknd, Ariana Grande

Hold You in My Arms – Ray LaMontagne

Pure Shores – All Saints

Dreams – The Cranberries

Ocean Eyes – Billie Eilish

Forever Young – Youth Group

So Here We Are – Bloc Party

Don't Dream It's Over – Fearless Soul, Rachael Schroeder

Chapter One

I've got an hour to kill before he arrives and I dump his ass again.

The breakup was a priority, and Lucie needed time to practice how she'd dump him. She'd tried ending their relationship the night before, but her anxiety had overwhelmed her. He wasn't paying attention to her anyway, too busy playing on his phone to hear. She shrugged. The end of her so-called relationship wasn't her main thought anymore.

Crowds blocked the path to the station exit. Strangers fumbled for tickets hidden in pockets or scrolled through the screens of apps on their phones to get through the barriers. An announcer reminded the jostling groups that the trains' doors would close thirty seconds before departure as swathes of birds flapped noisily through the open-roofed structure.

Her phone buzzed with a call.

"How did it go?" Emma, her younger sister, ignored the niceties as usual. "Did you get it?"

"I messed up, especially when they asked why I wanted to work for them." The hiss of trains leaving the station made it hard to hear, but the memories of the interview question was louder than any locomotive.

"I'm sure it wasn't as bad as you think. You worked on your answers for days. Even I know your answer was, 'Because you're market leaders in branding. Your customers and employees rate you highly, blah, blah, blah.'" Emma's southwest England accent was developing a slight Aussie twang, but it didn't make Lucie smile today.

"I didn't say any of that. I fluffed the interview for the role of my lifetime. I've dreamt of that opportunity for years. Every second was agony, and then I stumbled over the few words I spluttered."

Another train departed the frantic station as Emma's baby cried in the background. "I've gotta go, but it can't be as bad as you think. Nothing is. Before you go, what do you have to say?"

Lucie huffed into the phone. "I'm awesome. I can change the world."

"And you're going to tell Bradley that it's over before you waste any more of your twenties with him. I'll call later, okay?"

"Okay," Lucie replied.

"And remember," Emma said. Lucie could already hear the smile in her voice. "I love you like Dec loves Ant."

"And Ant loves Dec," Lucie replied, her heart calming. Emma hung up quickly.

Their shared declaration was a weird thing they'd done ever since they'd watched Ant and Dec as kids. It was also a way of saying that everything was okay between them and always would be.

Lucie recalled the moment they'd said it in the pouring rain on the family holiday after the worst argument they'd ever had. It was the same weekend her life changed forever—the weekend she met Chris, her first love with beautiful green eyes and dimples when he smiled.

Suddenly a grey-haired guy on his mobile barged into her. She wobbled on her heels.

"Hey," she shouted, giving him a swift elbow before regaining her footing and striding to the toilets.

After a crappy interview and an imminent breakup, it wasn't the day to piss her off. She faltered as the adrenaline from the morning dropped. She turned. Should she apologise to the guy for elbowing him? Maybe he was on his way to his firstborn's birth, or what if he interviewed her one day and remembered her as rude? What if she'd, unbeknownst to her, upset her interviewers in the past too?

She shook herself. The guy had ploughed into her, and he hadn't apologised, and her interviewers didn't know her. It was her inability to answer a simple question that had cost her the job. The "we don't want you" phone call was coming. Her heart sped as her thoughts escalated.

Screeching strangers surrounded her, and the roar of departing trains made it hard to breathe. Lucie gulped stale air as she threw herself at the toilet door.

Was an anxiety attack coming? She didn't sense the intensity of a panic attack; anxiety attacks were different. Was it the idea of confronting Bradley rather than letting the relationship peter out like she usually did? Her past relationships, if she could call them that, replayed in her head as she flipped on the tap to run cold water over her wrists. How many emotionally unavailable liars had it taken to push her to pick someone different? No, today her dream job had slipped through her fingers.

She stared at her reflection in the mirror. Her long blonde bob, which was a lot lighter since she'd had six inches whipped off, bounced against her shoulders. The new look was unnecessary for a job that she no longer had a chance of getting. She hissed a sigh, forcing strands up in the air.

She squinted at her reflection in the long mirror. Her long cobalt blue pleated skirt reminded her of the warm seas of Phuket that she'd swam in on her travels. What was the guy she'd had a fling with before he tried it on with her friend called? She blinked his image away, focusing instead on how well the colour of her skirt matched her eyes. Would she wear it again after today? Her white top showcased her tan from her recent trip to California for the annual family holiday. They'd come a long way since their early September weekends in a forest holiday resort.

What was the point of looking the part if she couldn't answer the big question? Her pulse was rising, and sweat beaded the back of her neck, dampening the bottom of the bob. Tears were threatening to spill. The cold water wasn't working.

She couldn't do it here.

"Keep it together, Lucie, and don't let the anxiety win," she whispered.

Taking slow, deep breaths, she ran her thumb in circles across the inside of her wrist instead. She didn't need to see her tattoo. The words were imprinted on her mind as well as her skin. Chris had been the one who'd given her the quote.

Be the exception.

When he'd shared those words with her, his green eyes bright and his dimples pronounced, she'd been an awkward seventeen-year-old who was scared of her skin.

With a soft sigh, she lingered on his memory. It was worn from the frequency with which she visited it. What was he doing now? Had he reached the greatness he thought was possible in her, or was he fumbling his way through job interviews too? Her life had changed dramatically, and his life probably had too. But she couldn't forget why they had stopped speaking. The time for explanation and reminiscing was long gone. He was the one that got away, the one she'd never forget.

Be the exception. He'd said that to her the weekend she fell in love with him.

Lucie glanced in the mirror, grateful that calm had returned. All the hallmarks of a dirty train station bathroom reflected back at her. Chipped ceramic and stained lino were no distraction from her lousy day. A pathetic *pfft* sound came from above, and now a spray of air freshener mingled with the urine smell that lingered longer than the passengers washing their hands.

Her phone vibrated with another call. But it wasn't Emma again. It was Bradley, her soon-to-be ex-boyfriend, once she built up the courage to dump him.

Her shoulders slumped, and a bit more of her heart broke away. Was this her future? Pointless conquests and meaningless connections? She gritted her teeth and gathered the courage to ditch him for good.

CHAPTER TWO

"**H**ey, babe. Are we still on for the Sidings Inn in an hour?" Bradley, her soon-to-be-ex yammered. He was barely a footnote in her story. "I might have to change the time. I've got a bigger priority. No offence."

She didn't expect him to wish her good luck for the interview, but did he remember that's where she'd been? The sooner he was out of her life, the better.

"I'd like to meet if possible because I've got stuff to tell you," she replied, offering hints for him to mention the interview.

"Okay. I can change her—I mean it, the meeting. Cool, cool." He was sleeping with someone else. He told her that week that he and Lucie were in an open relationship. When did she agree to that? Surely, the dumping was unnecessary? "Make sure there's a pint waiting for me when I arrive, yeah. I get proper thirsty around you."

His His laugh reminded her she should have dumped him before last night. When would she get past this issue of confronting people, especially men?

"Sure," she replied sarcastically. "I bet you'll want me to buy you lunch too."

"You know it, babes, although I'd rather chow down on you."

Her breakfast would have been threatening to splash on her interview shoes in a vomit explosion had she eaten any.

"Got to go, Bradley. Noisy trains." She hung up instantly. Emma's statement about wasting her twenties with Bradley hit hard. Every relationship in Lucie's twenties had been a waste of time. Was it because she picked the wrong guys, or was she incapable of genuine relationships?

Earlier in the week, Lucie had Googled the best places to dump someone in the city, not believing she'd have the strength to do it anyway. The Sidings pub was big enough that they could find a quietish corner but sufficiently public to stop him from suggesting break-up sex as a goodbye. Not that he'd dare. Now that the interview was done, she needed to rip off the plaster. As soon as lunch was over, they would be too. Wouldn't they? And even if they were, what then? Was she doomed to repeat her relationship mistakes because the only man she'd loved was from a teenage holiday or because her dad was an arsehole? *Maybe I'm a failure.* When she was at her most anxious and vulnerable, that voice appeared. It sounded a lot like her dad.

At least she had no chance of getting the job. She could have been living in the same city as Bradley. She'd wanted to move to Bristol for the opportunity to live somewhere that brought back memories of the good parts of her childhood and the chance to rewrite history as an adult in control of her destiny.

She was fond of this place where she and Emma once lived. But now, Lucie wanted to drink in bars after work with her new colleagues while adult strangers zoomed past on scooters. She longed to sit by the harbour as the sun set, to pop by a different street festival every Saturday, to laugh in hipster places where you'd eat sweet potato fries while playing overpriced table tennis. And in the city, there would be more men popping up on her Bumble account. Surely, they weren't all as ridiculous as Bradley?

Chris hadn't been like Bradley. *But you knew him for one weekend eight years ago, and he was eighteen.* The voice of inner judgement appeared again. Her memory of Chris sprung up repeatedly no matter who she was dating. Lucie had shared more of herself with him than with anyone since. That was what holiday romances were—a chance to be someone else or, in her case, the opportunity to be your authentic self with another person for the first time. She'd chosen not to hide the version of herself that was totally her.

There was another reason she wanted to move back to Bristol, and it was something she hadn't breathed to anyone. Chris lived here. Lucie had admitted it late at night after a couple of glasses of wine and, even then, only to herself. They may have met on holiday and had never seen each other again, but they grew up in the same city. She'd moved away not long after they met, but they never spent time together again beyond the forest holiday park.

There was a possibility he still lived here. It was ridiculous that there could be anything between them now, but what if they met again? Would it be like a Netflix love story or a rose-tinted memory where he couldn't remember who she was? Lucie shuddered at the thought of an embarrassing rejection. She and Chris once had something special, but it had been so long ago.

A gaggle of teenage girls filled the toilet. Lucie paused before squeezing out the door. Their high-pitched voices bounced off the worn tiles as they chatted about dating and makeup. Thank God those awkward years were over, especially with things like TikTok around now.

As she reached for the door, one of the girl's T-shirts caught her eye. Sequins in a rainbow of colours glinted from the top. A flash of memory hit Lucie hard. The Forest Café. Lucie had loved the café as a teenager and often visited it when she wanted time out from the busyness of the city. The ceiling resembled the night sky, and fake trees were positioned around the place. Sounds of a rainforest accompanied the space. The hidden location and the unusual décor meant it didn't get many customers, but it kept going somehow. Chris had talked about it too, and they joked about meeting up there one day.

Maybe it was the memory of those beautiful green eyes she hadn't been able to stop thinking about since she'd arrived in Bristol that morning or because she was back at the station with an hour to kill. Or maybe she wanted to be somewhere that once brought her joy. Pushing through the door out of the toilet, she made her decision. Hopefully, the café still existed, and she'd be able to look up at the stars.

Maybe her special booth would be free too. Once a day, around lunchtime, rainbows would appear on the table of her special booth. Lucie hadn't deduced what was on or around the table that made this special effect appear, but on sunny days, magic would happen.

The crowds in the station reduced during the lull between trains. With a sweep of her head, Lucie spotted the exit that led towards the café.

If she got the job, she might be walking past this station daily. Even when jammed with people, the commuter hot spot didn't faze her. The near anxiety attack was more about the death of her dreams than the busyness of the station. But the chances of getting the graphic designer role at Morphosis were impossible now, which also meant taking that crappy job in Glasgow at Invo. Today was her last chance to see if the rainbow still appeared on the table.

With a sigh, she brushed the back of her fingers across her tattoo and left the station. Slipping down a side alley, she thought about Chris again. Things had ended painfully between them, and yet, when university made her question her hopes, or when she was at her lowest after visiting her dad, she'd find the money to visit the café. She'd wait until her rainbow booth was free and fantasize about Chris, filling her head with ridiculous hopes that she'd bump into him. At her lowest, she longed to be the version of herself he brought out. Lucie hadn't been back to the café in years.

"It's still here." She gasped as the familiar green sign came into view. As soon as she stepped through the door of the Forest Café, the lure of roasting coffee beans hit her. There were changes; they sold alcohol now. Thank goodness, because today called for something a lot stronger than coffee. Other additions included a tank full of tropical fish in the middle of the room. There were fewer trees, and the sounds of catcalling monkeys had gone. The décor was a mess, but as she leant her head back, she smiled. The stars were still on the ceiling, glinting, reminding her of life's possibilities.

Would the rainbows still appear on the special table?

There were more booths now, but she glimpsed her favourite one in the corner. She stepped closer. It was occupied. Maybe she could sit nearby until it became free?

As she took a seat at a table, the person at the booth

stood. Was he leaving?

As he turned, her heart froze, and heat sped through her body like flames multiplying underneath her skin. Her stomach churned, and a tingle raced up her spine as she came face-to-face with the guy with beautiful green eyes and dimples when he smiled.

She gasped louder than she intended when he stepped closer to her table, instantly drawing his attention and stopping him in his stride.

"Lucie Smith?" he asked, his eyes wide and his voice shaky.

"Chris? Chris Jones?" she replied, trembling.

CHAPTER THREE

EIGHT YEARS EARLIER, FRIDAY

"**W**ho's excited?" her mum called out from the front passenger seat of the immaculate Ford Focus. There were no marks or sweet wrappers. Everything was as pristine as when Lucie's dad had bought the car eighteen months earlier.

"Can we have something else on the radio? I'm bored of classical, and I want to listen to Radio 1," Emma shouted to the front.

"You'd rather listen to something vapid that will rot your brain?" their dad replied quickly from the driver's seat. "I thought not," he said without allowing her to answer. "Classical it is then."

Emma rolled her eyes before her attention returned to her phone.

"One last weekend holiday and in a beautiful location," their mum tried again. The faux joy that made their mum's curls bounce up and down was too much. Emma had the sass of a fifteen-year-old but combined it with the intelligence to know when not to say anything hurtful.

"I'm excited, Mum," Lucie replied to keep the disappointment from clouding over her mum's face. It wasn't going to be an awful weekend, but it wasn't going to be the forty-eight hours of non-stop fun that their mum wanted them to believe it would be. Still, Lucie wanted her mum to smile. They were both trying their best. "We're going to have a great time and lots of fun."

Her dad huffed from the driver's seat before adding, "It will be the last fun you'll have for a while. You need to knuckle down this year, or you'll never get into university to study law. You know how competitive it is, and your grades aren't good enough."

Lucie bit her tongue, determined not to cause any problems, but her dad continued his lecture regardless.

Her phone vibrated with a message. Emma nudged her in the ribs. She was always sending texts of what she wanted to say when Lucie was victim to one of their dad's speeches. Emma was the only one other than their parents with her new number too.

Emma: *Do you want me to tell him I've got a massive hangover from Dan's party last night? It will change the subject from you quickly. And when are you going to tell him you want to study art and not law?*

Lucie shook her head while pretending to flick her fringe out of her eyes so that Emma would get her meaning. They were nearly at the roadside restaurant, and it wasn't worth a fight with their dad now. There were likely to be many more lectures that Emma could distract him from later.

"Don't shake your head at me. Once you get to university, you'll wish you'd listened to my wisdom," her dad continued sternly.

"Oh my God. I haven't told you about last night,"

Emma moaned, lengthening all her words in mock-hangover exaggeration.

Their dad gripped the steering wheel tighter. "Don't interrupt me, Emma." His voice was rising quickly.

"But it went off. This guy dared me to drink—"

"There's the restaurant. The Little Chef!" their mum exclaimed in an attempt to diffuse the escalating tension.

Lucie bit her tongue. Although it was probably a story Emma made up to exasperate their dad, she wanted to hear the ending. Lucie hadn't been to any of the local parties. Emma would take her even though she wasn't invited, but no one would want her there. Sometimes the kids from their school and the local boys' school went, but other times, groups from the local comp schools would go along. They all knew each other in passing. Emma told her that most people considered it a night to get drunk and fool around with someone random. For Emma, it was more about hanging with her mates and doing stupid stuff.

"You should have come to last night's. It was a party for those going to university. I know you don't go for a year, but you might have had fun," Emma whispered but not quietly enough.

"No parties for Lucie. Not that she'd know what to do. She'd probably be in the corner doing her homework, and no one would talk to her anyway," their dad muttered.

Emma undid her seatbelt dramatically with a roll of her eyes. The move showed the smiley faces and random drawings etched up her arms. The inkings often covered Emma's arms after parties. Apparently it was her way of planning her future tattoos. Emma was three years off eighteen and going to university, not that she had any intention of going, but that wouldn't prevent her from partying where and how she wanted. Lucie sighed despondently. She'd probably be too anxious around the popular kids and would end up telling everyone off for breaking the rules, and she'd never cover her arms with something that would last forever.

Their mum attempted to rouse the group as they got out of the car and walked through the car park to the Little Chef. "We will stop here for a short time, grab something to eat, and then head to the holiday village." She clasped her hands tightly as she aimed a meek smile at their dad. It was her standard pose when attempting to placate him.

"What else happened at the party?" Lucie whispered to Emma.

"So this one guy was off his face, and he had this massive row with this girl. Jess said it was his girlfriend. They're the coolest couple in their school. Then she got off with someone in front of him, so he jumped off the flat roof into the swimming pool."

"Seriously? Did he die?"

Emma stepped back and giggled. "No, of course not. Jess and I were preparing to use our lifeguard skills on him, but he was completely unharmed. Everyone thought he was so cool, but it was a real dick move. When he got out, he ran from the party, shouting that he would buy fireworks and celebrate being single. I've no idea what happened to him after that."

"He's probably in a ditch or riding a rocket to Uranus," Lucie replied, rolling her eyes.

"Isn't that what Fern in your year said when the teacher asked about her Christmas holidays?"

"No, she said she was riding a guy's anus, but the teacher pretended she heard differently. She heard right, though. Her face was bright red!" All it took was one look

17

at Emma to set her off laughing. It was a silly joke, but remembering that moment, how the teacher's voice hitched as she said Uranus, got her every time.

"Riding a guy's anus? Who says that?" Emma's laughter was bubbling over now. "And to a teacher, oh my God."

Their parents looked back at them with their eyebrows raised.

"I know," Lucie whispered. ""Fern, how did your Christmas go?' 'Oh, you know, Mrs. Titcombe, I was riding a guy's anus. Yours?'" Lucie held her hand over her mouth, but guffaws flowed out between her fingers.

"She said it to Mrs. Titcombe? The woman who still wears Victorian blouses? Amazing!" Emma was laughing so hard she'd bent double while still walking into the restaurant.

"What are you two laughing about?" their mum asked as they stepped through the door and waited for the server. "And stop bending over, Emma. This is not the time for your silliness. Your dad won't like it."

Lucie smirked but kept her mouth closed as Emma righted herself. There was still a cheeky glint in her eye.

The server reached their family, and as she guided them to their table, Emma pointed to the mural on the wall next to them. "Dad, Lucie and I are having a debate, and we can't remember what order the planets come in. What's that one next to Saturn? It's famous for its ring or something."

"Saturn is famous for its rings," he replied flatly. "It has seven rings."

Lucie hid her smiles behind her lips, unable to keep in the laughter for much longer, but Emma didn't stop.

"Interesting. I guess you can never have enough. But tell me about the other planet with rings, not Jupiter."

"Ah, you mean Uranus," he said, stopping them in the middle of the restaurant. Lucie held her breath to stop the laughter bubbling at her throat. "Uranus has many rings, and the inner rings are narrow and dark."

Emma opened her mouth as Lucie glared at her to be quiet. She knew what was coming. "So you're telling me that Uranus has a narrow and dark inner ring?"

That was it. The laughter was uncontrollable. Tears streamed down their faces as red splotches appeared on their dad's face.

"How dare you embarrass me. I wouldn't expect anything less from her," he replied, pointing at Emma. "But you, Lucie. This holiday is a treat, and you are showing up your mother in front of the whole café. She's been looking forward to this holiday for a long time, and she doesn't need to have it ruined by two silly little girls who find rude things funny. Now sit down and shut up."

Emma smiled as they sat, but Lucie felt the heat of shame creeping up her face. Everyone in the restaurant had heard him. She sat in her plastic-covered chair and fought the tears brimming in her eyes.

CHAPTER FOUR

Silence descended on the group. Occasionally Emma nudged Lucie's foot under the table, but she ignored her, refusing to make eye contact.

Her dad huffed and puffed next to her.

"Stop being silly, Lucie," her dad said, eventually returning to his reprimand. "You'll have to manage people having a go at you when you're a lawyer. For goodness sake, child. Now sit up straight and stop being a baby."

I'm not a child.

Lucie let out a noisy burst of air as she wriggled in her seat. The familiar pain that came from wearing shorts in the summer and sitting on plastic while sweaty made her squirm as she leaned back further.

"I don't want to hear any more about parties either. Weren't you and Jess swimming last night?" their dad replied.

He didn't care what Emma got up to. It was as if he'd stopped trying to make her behave when she hit thirteen and rebelled at his every request. Allowing her freedom was a deal they were both happy with. Lucie got all the pressure of being perfect instead, but she didn't resent Emma, far from it. She wanted a taste of that freedom just once.

"Technically, we were swimming, but not at the local

pool," Emma replied with a shrug.

"Well, you can't take Lucie. Even if the others wanted her there, she'd find a way to ruin it."

"Who's having what?" her mum whispered conspiratorially across the wooden table as she smiled broadly at her daughters, trying to appease everyone again. "Isn't this fun? We're lucky that your dad brought us here for lunch."

"It's a waste of money," her dad grumbled as he poked at minuscule crumbs that he'd revealed when he lifted the laminated menu from the Formica tabletop. Sun reflected off the plastic as he wafted it around. "As if I'm not paying enough for a weekend at the expensive holiday village. We could be having sandwiches in the car, but instead, I'm forking out for this."

Emma rolled her eyes and reached for the menu, but their dad whipped it away quickly.

"You don't need the menu. I'll tell you what you're having, and it will be the cheapest thing," he grunted. Due to his obsession with money, he'd picked the holiday village that was the closest, less than a ninety-minute drive away. He smugly told them it was so he could work in the morning and not pay too much for petrol. The real reason they stopped for lunch was because he hadn't allowed them time to eat at home or for their mum to prepare anything. Instead, he'd shouted at them to leave when he was ready.

"But, Dad," she cried out as he continued to hold it out of her reach.

Lucie sat with her hands folded in her lap as the father-daughter battle continued. Why did Emma fight him even though he always got his way?

"Behave, Emma. You're not with your friends now," he

said with the pointed stare he usually gave to end an argument. The skin around his eyes tightened, and he puckered his lips. Finally, he popped the menu back in its Perspex stand, officially closing the matter.

Emma winked at Lucie and mouthed, "Take it," behind her hand so that only Lucy could see. Lucie was sitting right next to the menu now, and it wouldn't take much to grab it. Lucie shook her head briefly, but Emma nodded in the direction of it again. Her smile and the light in her eyes made Lucie want to be the sister who had fun and went to parties. And after her dressing down, she wanted to best her dad too. Slowly she slid her hand across the table. She sucked her lips into her mouth nervously. Her heart beat a little faster, and she held her breath as her fingers pinched the corner of the menu.

She whipped it up quickly, smiling broadly at Emma.

But her joy was short-lived. Her dad nudged her, and the menu slipped out of her hand to the floor.

"What a surprise. Clumsy Lucie shows us up in public again," he shouted as a droopy-mouthed and sighing waitress in a bright red apron appeared at their table.

The familiar heat that filled Lucie's cheeks when her dad insisted on embarrassing her in public burnt her face. She glanced at her mum, who gave a wincing smile before inspecting her skirt.

"Pick it up then," her dad insisted. "This lovely woman is here to do her job, and you're getting in the way as usual."

Lucie scampered to her feet and picked up the menu, placing it in the Perspex holder so quickly that she knocked it again and grabbed it before it fell off the table. Unfortunately, it banged against the wooden sides before she righted it.

"Lucie, stop," he commanded with disdain as she sat down, dropping her head quickly but not before she caught the waitress's pitying face.

Lucie usually kept her hands in her lap to avoid knocking anything or doing anything clumsy. Why had she tried to outdo her dad?

Their dad ordered tap water and cheese and ham toasties for all of them before the waitress walked away.

"I want the toilet," Emma announced loudly. "Come on, Lucie, I need you." Lucie skittered to her feet.

"It doesn't take both of you to go to the toilet. Sit down before you break something, Lucie." Their dad nodded at her chair to enforce his point.

"I need help because I'm on my period, Dad. I wasn't expecting it today, and Lucie is my older sister, and she might have things to help," Emma replied before dragging Lucie in the direction of the loos.

Emma pulled her into the cubicle before forcing the seat down and sitting Lucie on it. She flipped the lock and then took both of Lucie's hands in hers. Where Emma's fingers were delicate, Lucie's were stubby.

"No wonder I'm the clumsy one. I don't glide; I waddle," she mumbled.

"Lucie, look at me," Emma implored her while squeezing her hands as she talked. "You are not clumsy. You don't get in the way, and you have nothing to be embarrassed about. He is the problem and not you. You're kind and caring."

Lucie took a deep breath, her hands trembling as she

gazed into her sister's eyes. How did Emma see her as that person when she couldn't see it in herself?

Lucie closed her eyes and took another breath as Emma continued, "You're amazing, and every day I remind myself how lucky I am that you're my sister. Okay?"

"Okay," she squeaked in response.

"That's a start. Now, what shall we do to kill time so that we don't have to listen to any more of Dad's droning?"

CHAPTER FIVE

Back in the car after an awkward meal where the waitress got their order wrong and ended up comping their meal, Lucie was still trying to behave. She silently sat up straight with her hands folded in her lap. But it didn't matter what her posture was like or how quiet she could be because her dad was offering his wisdom again, as he called it, or lecturing her, as everyone else called it.

"And the hard work won't stop after this year. You'll have to focus and achieve beyond expectations from day one of university, and that's the first degree. Those days were impossible, but I excelled. Hopefully, you will come close to achieving half as brilliantly as I did. Eventually, you will join my firm, where I'll work you twice as hard," he finished with a chuckle that no one shared.

She glanced out the window, trying to force his words from her overthinking mind. They were wedged in there anyway, but she wanted one weekend to forget the pressure she was drowning under. Numerous varieties of trees restricted her view of the blue skies that accompanied their journey down the motorway. Chirping filled the air as birds shouted their freedom from the skies. Lucie lowered the window slightly and breathed in the scent of fresh pine. It was a beautiful location, but her dad was ruining it like he ruined all holidays. The queue to get through the forest holiday park snaked out in front and behind them.

"God, give it a rest, Dad. Let her enjoy this weekend. She's going to be eighteen on Sunday, and she's spending her birthday with her boring family rather than drinking in town with her mates," Emma piped up.

As the firstborn, the family business rested on Lucie's shoulders. Emma didn't know what she wanted to do with her life besides travel the world. Their dad had abandoned his ambitions for her around the time she swore at his top client before throwing up in the golf bunker at a corporate family picnic. Emma had been seven, and the word she'd shouted was "arse," but their dad was adamant she'd vomited on purpose. She'd confessed to Lucie that she'd eaten a lot of sweets and was aiming for their dad's golf shoes when she spewed. As a result, she was off the hook for a career in law. Instead, he focused his attention and drive on Lucie. It was hard being the favourite of a pushy parent.

Emma's best mate, Jess, and her family would be sharing their lodge that weekend. Jess's dad was also a lawyer and friends with their dad, which left Lucie hanging around them like a spare part or spending the whole time on her own. She'd even brought schoolbooks with her, but they were worse than last resort. Lucie had been allowed to bring a friend along for the weekend, but there wasn't anyone. She didn't fit in at the all-girls private school she went to. The other students didn't bully her. They didn't even notice her.

Emma's phone buzzed, and she guffawed while giving their dad the side-eye with her baby blues. He narrowed his eyes in the rearview mirror.

"That's it. Hand your phones to your mother now," he demanded.

"Oh my God. Are you serious?" Emma huffed and puffed as Lucie turned hers off in preparation for the handover.

"You know our holiday rules, darling," her mum sang out from the front seat. Her mum was beautiful but often quiet. They were a happy family mostly. Her dad could have been a lot worse, and it was good he provided for them. That was what her mum told her. He set many rules and insisted they abide by them, but didn't every dad do that?

Emma's moans climbed an octave. "But that's for when we get to the lodge. This queue could go on for ages, and how can I tell Jess when we'll get there and—"

"That's enough, Emma. Pass your phone to your mum. You will get it back at the end of the weekend. This weekend is family time, so no phones," their dad replied sternly. Lucie handed her phone to their mum, who promptly slipped it into a lockable bag. "Well done, Lucie. Now tell me, Emma, why can't you be more like your sister?" He turned to glare at Emma as if that would add impetus to his point. Maybe it would have if he didn't say it to Emma at least once a week.

Sorry, Lucie mouthed to her. Emma shrugged. How could he want Emma to be like her? Unbeknownst to their parents, Emma helped the anxiety symptoms Lucie hid carefully from everyone around her. She wouldn't have made it through school over the last couple of years without Emma. She was everything Lucie wished she could be.

Lucie petitioned her dad. "My phone doesn't bother me because I've had it a week. Emma should be allowed hers for a little longer. What if Jess and her family get stuck in traffic?" She shifted against her seatbelt, pulling it away from her body. Her body burnt up when she disagreed with her dad. It was like she needed to say it, as her heart beat faster and nausea hit her belly.

Their dad stared at her through the rear view mirror. His thick eyebrows framed his annoyance. "You'll have to do better than that if you want to get on the debate team this year. You need to act less nervous too. Your body language doesn't scream confidence." At the shake of his head, her fingers trembled. Why couldn't she tell him she didn't want the future he'd dictated for her? "And don't forget that you owe me for getting you a new phone after you ruined your last one. You should be on my side." She'd dropped her phone in the full sink while washing up. He'd walked in as she'd been taking a break, and she'd been so worried he'd tell her off for doing nothing, or because she'd not cleaned the glasses correctly, that it slipped out of her hand and plopped into the water.

"Emma, phone now!" he shouted.

Emma thrust her phone in her mum's direction. "Fine! Are you going to put yours in now too, then, Dad?"

"Your attitude, young lady." There was another lecture coming. "It's disgusting. I blame your friends, but not ones like Jess; she comes from good stock. You've been spending time with girls who are on scholarships. I don't have anything against poor people aiming higher, but what I don't like is—what's that man's problem?"

They all slid forward as their dad slammed on the brakes. It had to be to make a point, as they hadn't been going more than a couple of miles an hour.

"You can't stop there to unload," he grumbled to himself. "He's in the middle of the road, Kathleen." He opened the door as he continued his rant, but in his haste, he'd forgotten his seatbelt. Suddenly he was yanked back against his seat, much to the amusement of his daughters.

"Girls," their mum reprimanded with a strain in her voice.

"What? We're coughing," Emma replied, elbowing her sister in the ribs. "Aren't we, Lucie? We've got a sudden cough, honest."

Lucie covered her mouth, but Emma's winks and giggles between fake coughs set her off again.

Finally free of the seatbelt, their dad launched himself out of the car and barrelled up to the stranger. He was no match for the guy, who had muscles that strained the material of his T-shirt.

"He's like Daniel Craig," their mum whispered as they all stared at the beefy stranger. Their dad insisted they watched James Bond films at least once a month, although he frequently extolled the classics and bemoaned Daniel Craig's portrayal of his favourite British spy. A couple of years earlier, he'd taken their mum to the cinema to watch Daniel Craig as Bond and then spent the rest of the week telling her why he was an awful choice for the role.

While the stranger now shrugging at their dad resembled a Hollywood muscle man, their dad's years of an exercise-free existence had taken their toll. He wouldn't survive the first punch if the argument ended in a fight.

"Quick, put down the windows. I want to hear this," Emma said gleefully.

Their mum wound down the window, and their dad's ranting carried on the breeze. "I wish he wouldn't do things like this," their mum lamented as their dad pointed his finger at the guy, who smiled calmly in response.

"He needs to practice his debating skills," Emma joked. Even their mum laughed at that one, although she hid it behind her hand in case their dad turned around.

Suddenly the passenger door of the stranger's Peugeot 206 opened, and another guy got out. This one was much younger and reminded her of the cute doctor from ER. Her mum made her and Emma watch it with her when their dad was working late. Lucie secretly enjoyed it. Their mum was always so chatty and relaxed during those programmes. The guy appeared the same age or maybe a little older than Lucie. His jeans hung low on his hips, and his fitted T-shirt hinted that he was lean, but maybe that there were muscles there too.

"Dad, our lodge is down there, number ninety-two," he called out with a hint of a Bristolian accent.

"Okay, Chris," the man listening to her dad shouted back. Suddenly some squirrels by their dad's car chattered and barked.

"They're totally doing an impression of Dad." Emma pointed out the gesticulating one to their mum, whose shoulders shook with laughter again.

Lucie turned back to the other window. The guy called Chris walked past Lucie's dad's car, a rucksack on his back and a tennis racket in hand. Lucie's eyes locked on his. They were bright green and sparkled like jewels. His hair was wavy and short. Was it soft too? As he passed her window, he looked at her, and the sides of his mouth turned up in a smile. Dimples appeared in his cheeks. Lucie smiled shyly back as a heat prickled her skin.

He continued walking past the car, and she forced herself not to turn and stare. Her cheeks were burning, and her belly fluttered. She held her breath and shoved her hands beneath her bum to sit on them and stop the need to pull at her clothes or ponytail. What was going on with her body?

"The little squirrel has beady eyes like your dad," her mum whispered loudly, but Lucie barely heard her. Emma and her mum's laughing got louder.

Even sitting on her hands, they twitched beneath her. She dropped her head and smiled to herself as the torrent of emotions rushed through her.

Her dad was back. The driver's door opened, and the rush of air flipped her ponytail and cooled the back of her neck. Sweat beaded her forehead, as a chill cascaded down her body.

"Right, he's going to move his car out of the way," their dad said while blustering his way back into the car. His face was red, his brows still furrowed. "What are you laughing about, Kathleen?"

"Nothing, just a cough," she replied while fake coughing between chuckles. Emma coughed along too, oblivious to Lucie's turmoil.

"I guess he didn't get a rocket to Uranus after all," Emma whispered in Lucie's ear.

"Who? Dad?"

"No," Emma replied conspiratorially. "That guy who got out the car. That's the one from the party who jumped in the pool. I can't believe he's here."

Emma quickly forgot Chris as she whispered something about the Daniel Craig squirrel in her mum's ear, but Lucie couldn't forget him.

Don't turn around. If that Chris guy sees you staring, he'll laugh at you.

As the car pulled away, Lucie turned to glance out the back window. Chris stood there, looking back at her with his beautiful green eyes. He waved with his free hand, his dimpled grin wide. She refused to move her hands and wave back. But as she stared at him, the tiniest smile crossed her face as their car disappeared away from him and farther into the woods.

CHAPTER SIX

"**E**ms, it's totally fine," Lucie said with a smile to Emma and Emma's friend, Jess. "I'm going to sit on the beach and draw. I've got my iPod and headphones. I'm happy. You and Jess have fun, okay?"

Heat bounced off the concrete while the sun warmed her bare legs. Sitting on the beach with her favourite tunes on repeat was the perfect way to spend the first couple of hours of their holiday.

Emma's lips twisted as if she was in an internal battle. Emma frequently went above and beyond for her loner sister, including the all-school trip to Alton Towers. Catty girls from the year above had laughed at Lucie when, pale and teary, she'd baulked at going on one of the "baby rides." Emma had shouted at the older girls and left the queue for the ride she'd been desperate to go on to take Lucie for ice cream.

Lucie would have liked to have a friend with her, but she'd never had friendships like Emma had or like television ones, and it left her with an aching hole in her heart. Was it wrong to want to be like everyone else? Popularity looked like a lot of fun, and it had to be better than the soul-crushing loneliness that swallowed her up when she sat alone at lunch or searched for a smile in her

33

direction when the teacher told the class to pair up. The other students who desperately attempted to avoid making eye contact made her want to sob, but no one would want to be her friend if she cried in front of them. Maybe it would be different when she got to university. One year to go.

"You're sure? Like really, really sure that you want to be alone?" Emma squinted against the sun of the late summer. Jess stood next to her, distracted by her fingers as she wiggled them around in the sunshine. Her fingernails had magnetic nail varnish on them, and it was all she'd talked about since she and her parents arrived at the lodge.

Lucie offered a nod and a smile to convince Emma. After Dad's endless lectures about preparing to study law, she needed the escapism she found through drawing. People streamed past them, heading to the variety of activities the holiday village advertised. A group of young teenage lads with messy hair cycled past, hollering at the pretty girls in short skirts giggling near the coffee house. If anyone did that to her, she'd hide all weekend. She wouldn't look good in one of those pretty skirts either. Her mum once commented on a dress that sat above Lucie's knee. Apparently, Lucie had oddly shaped thighs compared to the other girls at school. It was another thing for her to add to the long list of things she hated about herself. In this heat, she selected shorts that came to her knees in the hope that they were long enough not to draw laughter from strangers. She clenched her hands into fists. She didn't need to hide the rest of her legs, but she still looked sheepishly around in case anyone was smirking at her.

"Okay, if you're sure," Emma replied. She did her usual pause in case Lucie changed her mind. "But before we go, Jess, tell Lucie what you told me about that Chris guy."

"Oh yeah, if you see him, avoid him. He's a party animal and troublemaker. If he's here, then he will cause so much trouble."

"Like what sort of trouble?"

"Rumour has it"—Jess leaned in—"on the last day of term, he set fire to all his schoolbooks in the middle of the playground. Then he announced to his mates that he'd been sleeping with the maths teacher."

"No way is that true," Lucie replied.

"That's what started the argument between him and his girlfriend at the party, apparently," Jess said. She was such a gossip, especially as she believed everything she heard. "Stay away if you see him, because I swear, last night, he said he was going somewhere boring with his dad for the weekend and was going to cause as much trouble as possible."

Emma rolled her eyes. "Have fun at the beach and enjoy your drawing, Lucie. We'll be back in a couple of hours to pick you up before dinner."

Emma poked her in the ribs before hooking her arm through Jess's and heading towards the activity centre. Their laughter was loud as Jess gesticulated and Emma pointed out different things on their walk. Even from a distance, their confidence was unquestionable. Emma didn't hunch her shoulders or continuously wrap her hair around her fingers as Lucie did with her mousy brown ponytail. She hated these traits, and even when she tried to hide them, her dad repeatedly told her off for them as he did with all her faults.

Some days it was like her and Emma against the world. Emma was the only person who could talk Lucie down when her heart beat out of control, or she couldn't breathe or swallow during an anxiety attack. It was like playdough or clay was lodged in her throat, and she was terrified of suffocating. Each attack was more intense than the last. The terror that she would die, and her life would end as a failure, escalated the closer she got to the next school term and applying to university. The comedown from the attacks were usually spent at home cuddling a hot water bottle as tears and exhaustion overwhelmed her.

Lucie's breath caught in her throat. She squeezed her eyes tightly shut as she pulled at the end of her ponytail and counted slowly to ten. She wasn't having an attack but managing the anxiety that came with too many thoughts at once. What if she'd never be able to stop the attacks alone? She wouldn't survive a week at university without Emma. The one time her dad had witnessed the hint of an attack, he'd called it a child's tantrum, and now she let herself use those words too. Was she an out-of-control brat like he suggested?

The sounds around her slowly crept into her consciousness as the rushing in her ears quietened. Children giggled as they made sandcastles. The group of boys who'd been on bikes now sat with the girls near the water sports building. They pushed and shoved each other while laughing and shouting. Groups of teenagers and any activities that put you at risk, including water sports, terrified her.

Somewhere a stereo played "Firework" by Katy Perry. She liked the singer but couldn't tell anyone at school, as they'd laugh at her for not being into dance tunes like them. She liked all sorts of music. Wasn't it possible to like more than one genre?

Lucie let out a breath and focused on the water lapping against the artificial but realistic beach. A balmy breeze brushed across her bare arms, and she eased her feet out of her trainers and stepped onto the sand. The grains warmed her feet and filled the spaces between her toes. A sense of peace flowed through her limbs, and a sigh slipped from between her lips. She liked living in Bristol most of the time, but the proper sea was too far away.

Art college in Brighton was her secret dream. But her dad would get his way like he always did. If she performed as expected in exams, then this time next year, she would be preparing to live at home while commuting to Birmingham University every day to study law.

Her heartbeat rose again. After a deep breath, Lucie plopped down on the sand, popped in her earphones, and selected a playlist of old school tunes like the ones her mum made her listen to. Lucie had created it for that moment of reaching a place that gave her peace. "Champagne Supernova" by Oasis instantly warmed her chest.

Taking deep breaths filled her with the scent of ice cream, pancakes, and suntan lotion, and she let a sigh slip from between her lips. Then, with a smile, she opened her pad and began to draw.

Her breathing calmed as her pencil brushed the white paper. The vibrations in her fingertips eased the trembles that were so visceral when her dad challenged her. The sounds of gentle touches of lead on fresh paper grounded her, and after ten minutes of letting her pencil flow, a startling image took shape. It was a pair of eyes, but not just any eyes. They belonged to Chris, the troublemaker. Was he as bad as Jess made out? He'd been more rebellious at that party than she'd been in her whole life.

The possibility of bumping into him terrified her nearly as much as the group of teenagers whose happy yells were louder than her music. But the idea that she wanted to bump into him scared her more. *Just because he's attractive? You're so silly, Lucie.*

She'd had crushes before—on film stars, Emma's friends, and that guy, Jem, from the drama club she went to before her dad made her leave because she needed to focus on her studies. That night, she'd asked for Jem's email address, and he'd revealed he was gay and that he wanted a friend to email. That had been years ago. She'd never emailed him. It was accidental at first because she'd lost the address during an argument with her dad about how she wanted to return to drama club. Then, when she'd found it, she'd been too scared to message him. What if he believed she hadn't messaged for a month because she had an issue with him being gay? What if she had been the one person he'd told and then he felt rejected? She wasn't sure what to say, and he'd probably forgotten about her, anyway. She was too dull to be friends with a guy as cool as him and she felt guilty at least once a week that she'd never emailed him back.

In hindsight, all she'd felt for him was a silly schoolgirl crush. Silly was the word her dad used for her. Why did her negative inner voice sound like him?

All Chris did was wave at her. Another silly Lucie moment. He probably thought she was rude because she hadn't waved back. But the eyes on the page continued to captivate her. Lucie had lifted her pencil to add the dimples when, suddenly, sand burst into her face.

Instantly she began to choke. What the hell? There was sand in her eyes too. She yanked out her ear buds.

"Sorry." Someone bounded closer.

With her eyes tightly closed, she reached for her bag to grab some water, but it wasn't by her side. Panic welled up in her chest, and she attempted to rub her face. Where could her bag be? She couldn't let the sand into her eyes. How was she going to get it out?

Someone dropped down on the sand next to her as she reached to rub her eyes.

"Hey," a male voice said softly. "Don't touch your eyes at all, and definitely don't rub them. I'm really sorry. This is all my fault. I kicked the guy's ball way too far." He elongated the word "way" as if to prove a point. "I keep forgetting I'm not David Beckham. Have you got any water?"

"My bag," she replied, rasping from her heaving coughs.

"Okay. The first thing you need to do is blink a lot, and you need to cry so that tears can get the sand out."

"You want me to cry?" she asked. The stranger's hand brushed hers as he handed her the open bottle of water from her bag. His skin was hot and sweaty.

"I could sing. That usually makes people cry," he joked as she took in big gulps of water. His voice was gentle. "Maybe I could tell you some jokes and make you cry tears of laughter."

"Not if your jokes are like your football skills. If my eyes were open, I'd be rolling them at you right now," Lucie croaked with more confidence than she felt. At least her coughing had stopped.

Tears slowly ran down her face, and she tentatively opened her eyes, but they were still too blurry and sore.

"When you can open them a little wider, you need to do that weird thing where you lift your upper eyelid over the lashes of your lower lid. Then the lashes act like a windscreen wiper," he said, leaning closer. His scent of spice and sweetness reminded Lucie of the smell of the school hall when they had discos with the local boys' college. She should hate the smell of Lynx Africa—all the girls at school moaned about it—but she secretly loved it.

"How do you know this?" she asked anxiously, reaching for her upper eyelid. What if she accidentally pulled all her eyelashes out? Her stomach clenched and she baulked at the idea.

"Bad things happen to me. I've had several broken bones, cuts, bruises, and eye situations like this. I once threw up bile in class, and it splashed across the desk and got all of my mates in the face. It was so gross," he added with a chuckle.

Finally, her vision cleared. Lucie gasped. Chris was looming over her, staring at her, and all the teenagers she was scared of were standing close, watching too. He'd gotten sand in her eyes and now was making it a billion times worse. She was trapped.

CHAPTER SEVEN

With sandy tears still running down her face and, no doubt, blotches over her skin from coughing, shame filled her body. How long had the teenagers and Chris been looking at her? She must have been a freak to them with the way she reacted. Rage quickly took over and diluted the shame into something worse. This was how her dad responded to situations.

"You? You did this to me." She stood up and shoved Chris. Her face was burning with too many emotions she couldn't control.

"Hey, crazy," one of the teenagers shouted as they surrounded her. "He helped you."

"He caused this," she said from the middle of the group. It was as if she was suffocating from judgement. It forced her anger higher as her tears, a combination of the sand, her rage, and shame continued to flow. "I should have known it was you."

Lucie glared at him as her body shook. Everyone on the beach was watching now. They'd spend the whole weekend knowing she was the one who freaked out. They were probably whispering about her too. Her throat was tightening up again, and although she was burning hot, chills criss-crossed through her body.

Chris motioned for the teenagers to step away. "I'll

sort this out, don't worry. Thanks for letting me play footy with you."

They all nodded and mumbled "no worries" and "anytime" as they stepped away. The tallest girl stayed a little longer. She attempted to threaten Lucie with her wide-eyed stance and crossed arms. But Lucie's anxiety was snowballing.

It was humiliating. Lucie closed her eyes and tried to block everything, making the anxiety worse.

When she opened her eyes, the girl was gone, but Chris remained in his long shorts and bright blue T-shirt.

"It's okay; take deep breaths." He leaned in as if to hold her shoulders, but she flinched away.

"Get away from me," she grunted under her breath. "I should have listened to Jess and stayed away from you. You're trouble."

She grabbed her bag and walked across the sand, but he was next to her within moments.

"What does that mean? You don't know me, and you don't get to say I'm trouble. I only kicked a bloody ball. And who the hell is Jess?" He glared.

"My sister and her friend, Jess, have met you. We're from Bristol too. You have a reputation," she accused him between clenched teeth.

"You don't know anything about me other than I'm a shit footballer and that I can get sand out of someone's eyes. My pleasure, by the way," he added sullenly.

"How dare you turn this around on me." Lucie fumbled in her pockets for her ear buds. She needed to drown him and everyone else out with her music. "Where are my earphones and my drawing pad?"

In her haste, she'd left most of her stuff where she'd

sat. That was the issue with an impending anxiety attack; all other thoughts disappeared. Lucie and Chris turned to find seagulls pecking at her stuff.

Before she could decide what to do, Chris ran down the beach, flapping his arms and shouting at the gulls, "Get away from her stuff, get away!" He gave impressions of their screeches.

Laughter broke free from between her lips as Chris danced and shouted and shooed without any fear of how he looked or the attention he was getting. It was weird to go from anxiety to anger to laughter within a couple of minutes, but the spectacle in front of her was one she'd never imagined. She'd never witnessed the cool kids at her school do anything like this. Chris didn't care. Maybe the change in moods was due to relief too. At least she hadn't had a full-blown anxiety attack.

The gulls flew to the skies, squawking their annoyance, or maybe they were congratulating Chris on his good shooing skills. He flopped down on the beach and brushed the sand from her earphones as she joined him, needing a rest after her intense emotions.

Chris reached for her drawing pad, but she snatched it away and slammed it closed. He'd almost seen that she'd drawn him!

They sat in silence for a couple of minutes as she gripped her pad tightly. What was she suppose to say to hot guys? He was still trouble, and she shouldn't be talking to him. Emma and Jess would be annoyed, and he had that girlfriend or ex-girlfriend.

"You can say thanks, by the way," he grunted.

"For getting sand in my face?" she replied just as quickly before covering her mouth with her hand. Why did she say that? She never said what she thought. "Sorry and thank you."

His laughter surprised her. "Yeah, sorry about that. I tried to show off to those kids and got a bit carried away. I didn't mean to get you in the face. At least it means I got to talk to you."

What did that mean? Why were her limbs suddenly heavy? Her throat felt dry like sandpaper, and her stomach tightened. Although there were similarities to what had happened moments before and a week ago at the mention of her university application, it wasn't an anxiety attack.

Breathe, for fuck's sake.

"Oh, cool," she replied blankly. "And I didn't mean to kick off. It's fine. It's just…" It was what? It was just she was a massive weirdo when around people and was scared she might be having an anxiety attack? She forced a deep breath into her lungs.

"It's all my fault. I shouldn't have kicked off either, but I'm not trouble. I'm not." He paused, then shook himself. "Are we cool?"

"Yeah," she said quietly. What should she say to him? He was popular and hot, and she was the one people avoided sitting with at lunchtime.

Chris replied, standing, "I should go. I'm sorry."

Even with the things Emma and Jess had told her, Lucie still wanted him close. "No, it's okay. Besides, what will I do if the seagull comes back? They might try and take my bag next time," she joked, trying to hide all the thoughts spiralling through her brain. "I can be a bit of a freak sometimes, and I'm sorry I said you were trouble." Lucie shrugged. She'd discarded her pad to her side in the hope he hadn't noticed it before holding her hand out and patting the air to encourage him to sit back down. He sighed, and she struggled to conceal her smile as his eyebrows arched above his sunglasses.

"I can be a freak too, which is obvious. But being a freak isn't always a bad thing," Chris said as he sat back down and stared at the water. Neither of them spoke for a while. Lucie followed the sounds of the children playing nearby. Little children in mismatched swimming costumes and sunhats with ruffles showed their sandcastle creations to their mums. Radiant smiles eclipsed their bright faces. Meanwhile, the mums clapped and cheered with genuine excitement before grabbing their hands and dancing down the beach to the water with them. There was something about a beach that brought out the joy in everyone.

"What were you listening to?"

Lucie blushed but offered him one of the ear buds and pressed play on her MP3 player. Maybe music would make the moment less awkward.

"High and Dry" by Radiohead played.

"Cool," Chris mumbled.

As if suddenly aware of himself, Chris shifted in the sand. "How come your sister knows me?"

"My sister and her friend don't really know you, but they've seen you around back home. They said something about a party you were at last night," Lucie said so quietly she was surprised he could hear her over the waves.

"Oh, right. I don't remember much about that party," he replied with a shrug.

"You were drunk and jumped into a pool from high up after you and your girlfriend broke up, and then you said you were going to get fireworks… apparently," she added, realising she'd remembered way too much.

"Oh yeah. It was a weird night. Maybe I should have said I don't want to remember." He laughed without mirth.

"I shouldn't have said anything. I won't mention it again."

Suddenly the first few bars of a song by S Club 7 played, and Lucie snatched the earphones back. "I don't know how that one got on the playlist." Chris gave her a wary stare. Although her stomach was fluttering and she was conscious of the heat on the back of her neck, she didn't want him to go. "I'm Lucie Smith."

She held out her hand and regretted it instantly. They were strangers sitting on the sand; she wasn't interviewing him for a Saturday job at Superdrug. But before she could pull it back, he shook it enthusiastically. His skin was warm and a bit clammy. It was rough and smooth in different places. She wanted to study his hands so she could draw them, but instead, she pulled her hand back as quickly as he released it. Maybe she should go before he worked out how odd she was.

"I'm Chris Jones. How ridiculous is that? Our names are so forgettable. Chris Jones and Lucie Smith."

Chris Jones. She'd never forget his name, and she'd never forget him.

"What are you doing in your notebook?" he asked with a nod in the direction of her pad.

Was the sun getting hotter? She picked at her shorts before grabbing her ponytail and letting it fall through her hand until she was pulling at the end of it. The sun glinted off the water.

Oh no, please don't let him see that I'm sweating.

She fought the temptation to lift her arms and check. She squeezed her arms against her body in the hope that none of the possible smells would get out. Emma would have told her if she was someone who smelt bad all the time.

Lucie turned slightly in his direction but refused to acknowledge the art pad or look directly at him. "Nothing. It's just a bit of drawing," she replied, struggling to swallow past her tongue, which seemed five times bigger than it was when they left home earlier that day. Maybe she was getting ill? That couldn't happen. She was supposed to be back at school on Tuesday, and her dad wouldn't tolerate illness.

"Drawing?" His dimples returned. She caught his eye. His smile was wide, and instantly heat filled her cheeks. She took the opportunity to distract herself with the pad and hide her face. "You draw? I am so jealous. I wish I could draw. Please show me."

Her tongue was thicker now. She gave her hair another yank to avoid making eye contact. "No, no. I don't show anyone what I draw. It's rubbish anyway. I'm crap at drawing."

"Tell me three positive things about yourself," he said suddenly.

She did look at him then. His sunglasses reflected her face, and she fought the temptation to lean in closer to try and get a glimpse of his eyes beneath the lenses. "What?"

CHAPTER EIGHT

Chris, one of the hottest guys she'd ever met, wanted her to name three positives about herself. What was wrong with him? Sickness filled her belly as he stared at her. Lucie fumbled with her bag.

"Three positives about you. Come on."

"I don't know," Lucie stammered.

"I had to go to therapy when I was younger because of my mum. The therapist talked to me about reprogramming my brain. Every time you think or say something negative about yourself, you have to say three positive things. It makes you see yourself differently. So, go on, three positives," Chris said. She wanted to ask more questions about his revelation. No one had told her they'd been to therapy before, although there were rumours about girls at school. Fern, the most popular girl in her year, said Preena's counselling for her craziness "clearly wasn't working well" when she'd got teary in class. Although Preena's parents were in the midst of a messy divorce, it was Fern's snide remarks and ongoing bullying that made her teary.

"I can't think of anything. Is it meant to be this hard?" Lucie confessed with a sigh after a minute of silence.

Chris's dimples returned, and he lifted his glasses. She held her breath. "Yeah, at first anyway." His green eyes twinkled in the sunlight, and she couldn't stop staring at them. The green contained flecks of grey in them near the pupil. It was like staring into a green glass paperweight where different colours swirled depending on which part you were looking at and in what light. Her belly flipped, and sparks filled her limbs. "Can I suggest a positive for you?"

She nodded slowly. Her forehead was tight, and she fought to lower her eyebrows and soften her features.

"You're really curious," he said with a smile.

"What do you—how did you—is that a positive?"

"You're curious about people. I could tell from how you take in the things happening around us. Also, your face changed when I brought up therapy and my mum. I don't think you realise what your face reveals. And, of course, curiosity is a positive trait. Imagine if you weren't curious. You wouldn't be as good an artist, and I'm sure you're great. You wouldn't be interested in people, and you wouldn't want to learn about the world." That silenced her. He'd shone a light on one of the things she was awkward about and made it into something positive. "Now I want two more positives, but you have to say these two."

In her excitement, she blurted out, "I'm imaginative."

He grinned back at her. "Amazing. And the third?"

"And…" She drew the word out for a while. She ran through all sorts of ideas, but each one sounded negative.

I obey my dad, I'm quiet, and I like being on my own because I'm used to it.

Those weren't positives, and with every second that passed, she was sure he must be regretting talking to her. What kind of person couldn't think of any positives about themself? Emma would be able to do this easily. That was it! "And I love my sister. But then everyone could say that, and she is easy to love. Everyone loves Emma. Well, I'm sure some people don't, but they're dickheads." She'd rambled on a bit, but she'd said everything so quickly he probably couldn't distinguish her words anyway.

"You're imaginative, and you love your sister. I love those two positives. But maybe next time, be proud of the last one. It is a positive about you. You could have said you have great taste in music too. I love S Club 7. My mum used to play them all the time."

Lucie opened her mouth to argue, but Chris carried on. "We can work on the positives thing. Now, this pad of yours."

Perhaps it was his confession about therapy and his mum or the way he'd talked about Lucie, but excitement bloomed in her chest like a tiny rosebud offered encouragement. Slowly she lifted the pad and handed it to him. Her fingers brushed his that time. Were butterflies flapping in her belly? She'd read about it before in Doctor Who fan fiction, but wasn't that something you got with random people you had a crush on? Were you allowed to have butterflies with guys who chatted to you like they cared about what you said?

He leafed through the drawings.

Please let him like them.

There were various faces, some animals, and the odd celebrity or TV star. He nodded and smiled, commenting, "This is amazing," and "I love the way you've made them look" on a couple, especially when he recognised the celebrity. But it was when he reached the last page of drawings that Lucie held her breath.

"Hold on. How have you drawn these?" Was he annoyed?

She took a quick breath and got ready to be shouted at. "It's from when I saw you earlier. I draw faces that stay in my head. I don't need the person in front of me," she replied shakily.

"Sorry, they're like my mum's eyes. I thought you'd drawn her eyes, not mine, which makes no sense. It reminded me of the way they'd crinkle at the edges when she'd kiss me goodnight or when I did something that made her proud." His gaze was wistful, and for a moment, she allowed herself to study him. It was as if he was lost in a world of memories. Suddenly he carried on. "Anyway, you're an awesome artist. I wish I could draw like that." Didn't he realise he had his mum's eyes? When had he last seen her? Her drawing was of his eyes when he'd waved at Lucie as she stared out the back window of the car.

"I could show you how to draw something simple," she replied with a shrug.

He opened his mouth wide and breathed in deep and quick like he might pass out. She blushed at the idea of giving him mouth-to-mouth. "Seriously? Oh my God, please, oh great and wondrous one."

Lucie giggled at his enthusiasm.

"And then you have to draw me and sign it," he followed up quickly.

"No chance." But she imagined how she'd shade his wisps of brown hair and how difficult it would be to recreate his dimples.

"I have to have a Lucie Smith original before she becomes a world-famous artist. Please, Lucie." He took her hands between his and flooded her body with warmth. A chill chased it around her limbs and made her shiver. How was that possible? "Draw me like one of your French girls."

Laughter bubbled up in her throat. She had an

embarrassing laugh—Fern at school had silenced her with that revelation a couple of times—but at that moment, she couldn't prevent it from escaping from between her lips. Chris's chuckles drew her attention to his dimples. How was she sitting there making these embarrassing sounds with such a fit guy?

"You did not quote *Titanic* at me?" she asked between giggles.

"Be glad I didn't add—"

"Don't you dare," she squealed before they laughed so hard, they gasped for breath. He squeezed her hands, and she nearly gulped.

Over the next hour, she taught Chris to draw eyes until he could do them in all shapes and sizes. Occasionally her belly butterflies would flutter to remind her that she was sitting close enough to breathe his scent. His fingers would brush hers as she showed him how to tease out details like eyelashes or add shading. She willed her pupils to not dilate when he stared deep into her eyes to feather the patterns of her iris. Sharing her skill with him gave her a focus and made it easier to be in his company. Her nerves settled slightly, and she barely touched her ponytail.

Although she enjoyed giving him a masterclass, she loved it more when he posed for her. It allowed her to study him without feeling self-conscious or intrusive. He had an odd blemish near his hairline and a tiny brown mole on his neck. The lightest of freckles covered both his cheekbones, and she resisted the temptation to get close and inspect them.

"I've got this weird bump on my nose. Touch it," Chris urged. His eyes were wide as he pointed energetically to his nose.

Lucie fumbled through her words. "I don't need to." She swallowed her fears. "Are you sure I can?"

He nodded enthusiastically. Lucie held her breath and brushed her finger gently across his nose. She didn't combust into flames or get called a freak. Chris wasn't a god with skin made of gold or a superstar too beautiful to allow someone like her to get close. He was an ordinary person.

"I busted my nose when I was six. Mum was having one of her off days. On days like those, she refused to leave her bed. She'd tell me to go and play quietly like a good little boy, but that day I didn't. Do you remember *Gladiators*?" He didn't wait for her reaction. "My dad was a big fan, and we had loads of episodes on DVD, and I would watch them all the time. That day I was standing on the coffee table in the middle of the living room. There I was, kitchen broom in hand, proclaiming that I was the greatest contestant the show had ever had. I jumped and spun while imagining I was in a battle to the death against Wolf. Suddenly I waved my broom high in the air. It caught on the lampshade, and I flew off the table, smacking my face on the television stand. There was blood everywhere."

Chris told his story enthusiastically and held Lucie mesmerised with each twist and turn. What did he mean by his mum's off days, and who had patched him up after the fall? "You have to include my dimples in your drawing." Attempting to talk while smiling broadly to show his dimples gave him an exaggerated puppet face effect.

She returned to her pad, pushing away her questions, and drew lines to create his dimples.

He pointed to his dimples. "You have to admit they're my best feature."

"Stop talking," she replied with a smile.

"I won't stop until you admit it," he insisted as he pointed again to his dimples. Lucie pursed her lips to prevent herself from laughing. "Say you'll include them. Please, lovely Lucie. Please." He drew out the word until she couldn't stop herself and giggled.

"That's a yes then?" he asked, the big grin still on his face.

"Yes," she replied, shaking her head and laughing louder when he punched his fist in the air in celebration.

CHAPTER NINE

As they sat on the sand, occasionally singing to the Rihanna songs filling the air from a group of twenty-somethings playing their radio on the beach, Lucie drew. She tried to focus on perfecting the oval shape of Chris's face and the soft cupid's bow of his lips, but his attention span didn't last long enough for posing. Repeatedly he made a noisy hum to attract her attention, and when he caught her eye, he made a silly face at her. How could one face get in so many positions? Her favourite funny pose was when he squidged up his face and stuck his tongue out simultaneously. Even then, he was cute enough to make her belly flip.

"Tell me a bit more about you?" Chris requested once he'd settled into posing again. He jumped from silly to serious, and she longed for him to fancy her. He made it easy to have fun and to trust him too. "What are your plans after you finish your exams next summer?"

"I'll be going to Birmingham to study law." A lot of the families had left the beach by now. The late afternoon slid quietly into the early evening.

"Not art?"

She squinted at her drawing as if it required her full attention as she shrugged. Chris saw right through her.

"What made you pick law instead of art?" he pressed. "I think you'll be amazing at whatever you want to do."

"You don't know me," she replied, glancing at him.

He shrugged. "True, but you managed to take me on earlier. So why law?"

"You know, stuff." She nibbled at her lip, hoping he'd drop the question, even as she contemplated telling him the truth. He pushed on.

"Lucie, you don't have to tell me if you don't want to. I get it. But I won't judge you, whatever you say, even if you tell me it's so you can become The Lawyer, the head of a gang of law-based crime fighters," he joked.

How did he put her at ease so effortlessly? His earlier vulnerability made her want to share. "It's my dad. He wants me to do law. His plan is for me to join the family business. He bought me a solicitor wig for my thirteenth birthday. I've tried to say I don't want to do it," she replied. But was that true? She behaved like a good daughter and tried to keep the peace as she'd been taught to. "I'll be rubbish at it. I can't debate. I hate debates." She sounded like a child moaning about being made to eat sprouts for dinner.

"Why do you hate debates?"

It was a simple question, but the answer revealed her weaknesses. She kept her head down and her pencil moving as she replied, "No reason, I just hate them."

He raised his eyebrows as he studied her. The simple reaction sent heat rushing up her face. Lucie rested her pencil between her lips and stared at her notepad. Occasionally, she'd roll the tip of the pencil around the edge of her mouth. It was another one of her nervous habits. Chris's eyes were on her, and she didn't need to look up to know. A bead of sweat dripped down her chest.

"Why haven't I seen you at the parties?"

The question caught her by surprise. He was tricky to predict. "It's not my thing." To avoid eye contact, she pretended to busy herself by inspecting her pad. But when she looked up at him, there was something new in his eyes. Why was he staring at her lips like he was fascinated by them? "Besides, we wouldn't chat, and you wouldn't notice me anyway."

"That's a weird thing to say."

The atmosphere was suddenly uncomfortable. Lucie hesitated as she considered reaching for her bag to pack up.

"I didn't get fireworks, by the way."

"What?"

"Last night. I didn't get fireworks like I said I would. I remember vague bits. I ended up outside my school and thinking about what I'm doing next with my life. Everyone reckons I'm a troublemaker, but I like having fun. Life is too short to be perfect." He ran his fingers through his hair, messing it up. "I'm good to my dad, and I do most of my work, so what does it matter?"

Was he trying to justify himself to her? Why did he care? "I guess. But don't you want to be the best version of yourself? Like don't you care what everyone thinks of you?"

He shrugged. "Sometimes. Like I do stupid stuff because it gets a reaction and makes people laugh, but it doesn't mean anything."

"But what if it means people don't respect you, or you get told off, or you miss out on opportunities because people don't trust you?" Lucie forgot her drawing as she waited for his answer.

"Is that why you do things? Do you care more what others think about you than what you think?"

Lucie shrugged, but heat crept up her neck, and her fingers trembled. Was an attack coming? She'd done everything to avoid confrontation. "I'm not sure," she replied quietly. If she lived as he did, she'd have to deal with daily fights with her dad. He would undermine her at every turn. "Look, the reason I don't like debates and the reason I hate this conversation is that I get nervous when I have to talk about my thoughts in public. I go bright red when everyone stares at me. I can't think quickly on my feet. I don't like it when people speak to me aggressively or are confrontational. I'm rubbish at explaining things, and I hate being wrong, laughed at, and humiliated." Her words ran away from her. Sickness churned in her belly, but it was worth it if it meant changing the subject and not arguing with Chris.

"Why didn't you say that before? Your art is amazing. It's a shame you're not getting to use your gift and going into law instead, but I'm sure you've thought through your decision. I'm guessing you think things through a lot."

Was that a back-handed compliment? A blush crept up her neck, and she nearly yanked on her ponytail, but instead, she focused on her pad. "Okay."

They sat in an uncomfortable silence, although sounds surrounded them, including shouts and giggles from the teenagers burying the youngest lad of the group in the sand. Seagulls fought over the sandwich crusts left by the children who'd now departed with their families for the lodges. The battle was intense as more gulls joined the pair, each fighting for a couple of crumbs. It was survival of the fittest until a terrier escaped its lead and ploughed onto the beach, swallowing the crust whole before barking at the departure of the birds. It was back on its lead in seconds. The owners eventually dragged the dog off the beach as the remaining toddler clapped his hands in glee at the spectacle.

"It's like being back at school or work," Chris said over the busy beach sounds. "I work in a supermarket part-time, and there was this one time when we were selling beef unbelievably cheap. These two women were arguing, and one of them was threatening the other with a handbag. The one with the handbag shouted that her husband loved beef. The other woman said that she knew that because he'd been getting it and more at hers. It turned into a rolling around on the floor fight, which I had to break up. I got punched in the face that day, but it was worth it because they quietened down and apologised after that."

She wasn't sure if he told the story to ease the awkwardness or because he didn't like silence. "How about you? You've finished school and got your results, right? What are your plans?" she asked.

"Yeah," he said, tipping his head from side to side as if he was stretching his neck. Sun glinted off his tanned skin. Lucie swallowed and sucked her lower lip into her mouth. How warm would his skin be against her fingers? "I'm off to university in a couple of weeks. I'm going to be studying psychology, but don't ask me why. I have no clue."

"You're not sure why you're studying psychology?" Imagine not having your subject choice forced on you from an early age. She'd never had a choice.

"Yeah. Like should I jack it all in and work instead? The managers at Tesco are always on at me to work full-time, but going to university will make Dad happy. It's not that he wouldn't be happy with whatever I chose, but he's

59

fought hard to give me a good life since Mum left, and I don't want to let him down," he said with a shrug.

"I get what you mean." She sighed. If her dad didn't make her go into law, would she apply to do art, or was she using him as an excuse? Arguing with her dad and going against his wishes wouldn't make life easy for mum. She couldn't let her down.

"But you have a skill." His eyes sparkled. The warmth rushed through her limbs again. It was a struggle to keep up with him.

"Art?"

"Yeah, you could do something amazing with that. 'Be the exception.' So many people are doing the right thing or the wrong thing for the sake of it. They meander through life and hope they get to the end with loads of money or status or power. You could do something with your art. 'Be the exception.' Don't let fear get in your way. Please don't let anything hold you back."

They stared at each other, and her heart beat faster. It wasn't like an anxiety attack though. Instead, it was like her whole world was about to be turned on its head, and he was keen to join her and would hold her hand through the journey.

His Adam's apple bobbed in his throat. She moistened her lips with her tongue, and his eyes dropped to her lips. Her pencil rolled down the pad into the sand, and she snatched it up, breaking eye contact.

"Show me the drawing then," he said, leaning close. His breath teased her neck as he tried to sneak a look.

"It's not very—" He raised his eyebrows, and she quickly said, "It's not very, umm, finished."

"Ha! I knew you were going to say that it wasn't very

good, but you got away with it this time." He held the pad between his hands and beamed. His dimples were as deep as the water that lapped at the edge of the artificial beach. He was beautiful. "You're an incredible artist. I wish I were as good as you at anything, although you have a rival for drawing eyes now."

"Thank you. And yes, you'll be the Da Vinci of eyes," she replied with a giggle. She spun her pen on her finger. His proximity was welcome, but she couldn't stop fidgeting.

He leaned in closer. His deodorant smelt spicy and woody all at once. Her head went fuzzy, and she held her breath. He tucked a few loose strands of her bangs behind her ear. Lucie shivered and excitement flared. Was he going to kiss her? Did she want him to? No way did he fancy her. She wasn't cool enough for him.

"You accepted a compliment. I bet you don't do that often," Chris said softly in her ear. He had been a stranger a couple of hours ago, and yet he knew her so well. But what if he was messing with her because he was bored? His voice was lower as he whispered again, "You're nervous, Lucie. Why is that?"

Was he teasing her? She held her breath as his hand reached for her fringe again.

"Hey, Lucie. We've got to get back for dinner. You'll never guess what we won." Emma and Jess came bounding up to her. Lucie and Chris reared away from each other. "Why are you talking to him?"

Of course Emma would say exactly what she thought.

"I… We got chatting on the beach. He saved my earphones from the seagulls," she replied meekly.

"I'm Emma, Lucie's sister," she snapped before thumbing in the direction of Jess, who was gazing intently at her outstretched tongue. It was blue. She must have downed several cups of her favourite drink, raspberry slushie. "This is my mate, Jess. We've seen you at parties."

"Yeah, I recognise you," he replied with the same enthusiasm that kept Lucie grinning from ear-to-ear all afternoon. Emma's attitude hadn't dulled his energy. "What's the time?"

"It's six o'clock," Emma grunted, looking him up and down with a furrowed brow.

"I've got to make dinner." He forced his feet into his trainers, but he was tripping over them because he was trying to return Lucie's pad to her. "Can I have this masterpiece? I can't wait to put it on my wall."

"It's not finished yet," she said as he danced around her.

"You'll have to meet me again tomorrow so that you can finish it," he responded with a beaming smile.

"You don't have to see him if you don't want to," Emma jumped in as if he wasn't there.

"I…" Did she want to spend another day being this nervous? *And this happy.* The voice inside her saying those last three words didn't sound like the one that made her feel less than she was. But what would Emma say?

"It doesn't matter," Chris replied, shoving his feet a little harder into his trainers. "I've got to go. You have a good weekend."

He ran from the beach.

"But—" she said but he was gone. What was the point anyway?

"Was that Chris? He is so hot," Jess said, catching up with the conversation. "I bet his girlfriend is gutted she dumped him. I heard it was to do with him going to university." Hadn't Jess and Emma said it was to do with him sleeping with a teacher?

"Tell us as we run. We've got to get back in fifteen minutes, or Dad will cancel bowling tonight and make us listen to his reason for cancelling it for the rest of the evening. I want to hear everything about Chris!" Emma said as Lucie forced her trainers on, and they set off on their run back to the lodge.

I should have said I would meet him. Why didn't I say anything?

CHAPTER TEN

Luminous pink and green balls slid down the lanes, racing to get to the pins. Neon lights flashed across the shiny alley before highlighting parents' smiles and little kids crossing their fingers. Would their skittles drop this time? It was always party night at this forest park entertainment building. Bowling should have been fun. But it wasn't tonight for Lucie and her family.

"A friend of a friend saw him get a tattoo off another drunk guy at a party once. I didn't see it, but his thigh has a scar from that night," Jess whispered in her ear. The rumours about Chris came thick and fast. Where did he find the time to do all the things he'd allegedly done? Jess was more vocal than Emma, but the message was clear: stay away from him. "And didn't he get caught getting a bj from his girlfriend and her best mate in the school science lab? Like who would do that?"

Was it possible to get a bj from two people simultaneously? "During the lesson?"

Emma laughed. "It wouldn't surprise me based on what I've heard about him."

Why was he nice to her if he was such a bad boy? From what Jess and Emma had said about his friends, including his girlfriend, Lucie was nothing like them.

Emma nudged her. "Look at Dad."

Their dad was inspecting the lane floor for bumps. "I knew it. My bowling was fine for a good quality lane, but I can't help it if the alley is substandard." His face was blotchy, and he made the noise of a strained groan as he raised himself from his crouching position.

Every day Lucie found a new reason to dislike him. Some days she had several.

Did the venue have an escape route? Would anyone notice if she sneaked off and sat in the toilet quietly for a while? Public loos were often her safe space. No one usually bothered her there, and sometimes at school, she could hide on a closed toilet seat for ten minutes without anyone noticing.

On every lane, balls rumbled up the machines as outdated pop music played in the background. Her mum mouthed to B*Witched when her dad wasn't watching.

"Come on, Dave. You can do better than that," Jess's dad, Steve, shouted over from his lane.

Her family was on one team, and Jess's family on another. Nothing mattered more to the men than the win.

Her dad bristled but accompanied it with a fake smile. "As I said, the problem was the lane. Also, as the score shows, my family is beating yours, mate." The trash talk was always the same when they got together. They were rivals in business and life.

"Because your wife is carrying you. Thank goodness for you, Kathy." Steve and Lucie's mum had gone to school together, and he'd called her that ever since. Shortened names niggled Lucie's dad, especially her mum's name. Was Steve doing it to make her mum laugh, or was his aim to piss off her dad? Her dad gritted his teeth and glared.

"Lucie is letting our side down," her dad said, nodding

in her direction. "She's been daydreaming through every go."

Why did he have to be so passive-aggressive? If he could make a dig, he would. If they were struggling, or something wasn't right, caring dads chatted with their daughters and found ways to encourage them, unlike Lucie's dad. She used to enjoy bowling, but every family night at the bowling alley, Lucie's dad would mention how bad she was at it.

Instead of saying something, she pulled the sleeves of her sweater down. At parents' evening, her psychology teacher had explained that it was a way of hiding a small part of herself from the world and that she would benefit from being more confident. Why did everyone have to tell her what was wrong with her?

"Maybe I need a different ball," she said loud enough for her dad to hear. It wasn't quite standing up for herself, but it was an improvement. Did "be the exception" mean acting like that too? Those three words reminded her of Chris. Suddenly the anxiety from managing her dad disappeared and was replaced with the awkwardness that came with remembering Chris. A weird sponginess spread throughout her body. Whenever she thought of Chris, she'd smile before her mood quickly dropped. So what if he'd been kind to her? He'd also been the same guy who got into trouble and couldn't be trusted. It was attraction and nothing more. She had to trust what Emma said about him. But if she couldn't be friends with people different from her, she wouldn't survive university. People there would ignore her like the girls at school did.

"She's daydreaming again. Earth to Lucie!" Her dad's voice cut through her daydreams.

"Huh?"

"Huh? You're supposed to say, 'Pardon.'" He laughed at her. "Why do you embarrass me in front of my friends? I'm never going to convince Steve that you'll be a great lawyer if you talk like that."

Her face burnt as all the adults stared at her. She yanked at her sleeves again.

"It's my go," Emma said loudly enough to draw everyone's attention. And then she grabbed the ball, eyeing their dad to make sure he was watching, and dropped it on the lane and walked away. She hadn't lined it up or tried to roll it but dropped it and walked off. It was such an Emma thing to do. Lucie hid her smile behind her hand so she wouldn't get in trouble for enjoying Emma's performance.

"I'm off to find a different ball," Lucie shouted, her oversized bowling shoes slapping the floor as she retreated in haste.

No one noticed her go. Steve bent over laughing, and her dad was fuming and stamping his feet while Emma shrugged in his face.

Lucie's thoughts returned to Chris. She hadn't stopped thinking about him since they met. More than once, her mum caught her daydreaming, and when nudged for an explanation, she'd pretended she was planning her stationery for school. But in truth, Chris's green eyes and dimples pierced her thoughts. And what was that other feeling? It was like when a sex scene came on the television. She'd watched a teen drama that everyone at school talked about alone in her room one night when her family believed she was asleep. The teenagers in it were her age, and they went to massive parties and trashed houses, and everyone had sex. One scene stood out. Two of the characters had sex at college on one of the desks while the teachers were in assembly. Lucie watched that scene a lot. Was that what she should be doing with guys? Her family didn't talk about sex. She'd asked Emma about it a couple of times, but it was the one thing she wouldn't say much about. No one at school talked to her, so she couldn't ask them. What was she meant to feel?

Lucie stared at the racks of spare balls. The air was full of weird and wonderful smells, like shoe disinfectant spray mixed with freshly cooked hotdogs and yeasty beers. She held her breath, but the smell got in anyway. It brought back memories of "jokey" arguments, usually between Steve and her dad, from nights like these. The teenagers from the beach were on a nearby lane. They laughed and joked, cheered each other on when one of them bowled, and whooped and hollered when someone made a spare. They were happy together, but Lucie looked away so they wouldn't catch her staring.

A woman suddenly appeared in front of her. With her skinny jeans and perfectly wavy hair, she displayed middle-class perfection. The small child hanging off her hip didn't detract from her style as they sucked on her colourful scarf, which Lucie had seen on at least four other women at the bowling alley. "Are you okay? You're the one that had a meltdown on the beach earlier." Heat crept up Lucie's cheeks as she attempted a response. Even in the middle of a forest holiday park, the same faces were always there.

"Yeah," she replied, looking anywhere but at the woman in front of her.

"Darling, it's Joshua's go," a man called out from the nearest lane. He was wearing the same smart jeans and checked shirt as every other dad in the place. As he said the boy's name, several children looked over. Was every boy here called Joshua? Lucie's eyes flicked to the screens, where the name Joshua was emblazoned on at least three of them, and Daisy was repeated several times too.

The woman returned to her lane, where Joshua got ready to bowl, commanding both parents' attention, who took turns sipping white wine. Every lane was the same: white middle-class Stepford family of two parents and two kids. The village was supposed to be a retreat from the world, yet the whole place was stifling. *I want to be free.* But free from what? Her family, school, herself?

"Whoop, whoop!" The teenagers were celebrating again. The smallest guy in the group got a strike, and the girl who'd stared Lucie down earlier was breakdancing in celebration. What would it be like to hang out with them? Was the atmosphere different for them because they were here with friends?

Fear of a lifetime of loneliness kept her awake some nights, but sleep could be worse. She had a recurring dream of getting to university and enjoying a night at the pub surrounded by friends. As she was laughing with her best friend, someone would walk in and tell her she didn't belong and that no one liked her. They'd make her leave. What if she got to university and was crippled by anxiety? There would be no Emma to rescue her then. "Be the exception" sneaked into her thoughts, but she batted it away.

Lucie focused on the balls in front of her and not the suffocating atmosphere of the entire entertainment building. The balls sat in rows of colours and sizes. Which one was best? It would be easier to throw if it was a lighter ball, but would that make less impact? The heavy ones powered all the skittles down, but not if you couldn't roll them properly.

A shiver covered her neck. Was someone watching her? Suddenly there was a tap on her shoulder. Was this another person ready to share their opinions on her beach antics? She turned her head, but there was no one there. Was Jess or Emma messing with her?

"Surprise," Chris said from her other side. His goofy smile brought butterflies to her belly. Her mouth went dry, and she winced at her reaction. "Sorry, did I freak you out? I wasn't sure how to say hi without making an idiot of myself," he added.

The smell of burgers and Lynx Africa wafted to her nostrils as she tried to find her voice.

"Please forgive me, Lucie." His smile was gone. With a furrowed brow, he was unbelievably cute. *Whatever you do, don't say that out loud.*

What should she say? Her silence had gone on for so long that she'd make it weird, whatever she said, but being silent wasn't good either. But no words came out of her mouth. *I want to meet him tomorrow away from everyone, but I can't say that because… because…*

"I should go. I'm sorry for being odd. That's what my teachers called it, 'Chris and his odd ways.' I should have known you didn't want to be around me. I guess you heard some stories about me from your sister. Anyway, I'm going to head off, but you have a fun evening," Chris said softly. The butterflies in her belly were flapping out of control now. She had to prevent him from leaving.

Chapter Eleven

"**B**alls," Lucie shouted abruptly,

Chris stopped suddenly, and his mouth dropped. "Balls?"

"Bowling balls," she said, recovering quickly. "I can't work out what bowling ball I need. I'm crap at bowling."

"You said a negative about yourself. I need three positive things right now," Chris replied quickly. He pointed at her, but not in a threatening way. Instead, he was like a teacher that wanted to make you laugh while expanding your knowledge on something significant.

"I'm good at drawing, I'm curious, and I nearly answered my dad back after he made a dig," she said quickly.

"You can't use curious again." He smiled with a wink. "But well done on the dad one. Good for you. In terms of the balls, let me help."

She forced back a giggle at the idea that he was offering to help her out with balls. *You are so embarrassing. You didn't find that funny?* Her inner voice asked annoying rhetorical questions too. It had a point, though. Thank goodness she hadn't laughed out loud. He would have called her a kid.

Chris jumped straight into telling her about the balls.

He shared knowledge in a way that wasn't condescending or passive-aggressive. He helped her try different sized bowling balls and gave her pointers on the best stance and position and how to move her arms. She was learning quickly, and she'd retain it too. He was fascinating and informative yet made it practical. It was more than she could have asked for. Was he aware he had this skill in sharing knowledge? Chris and his dad went bowling once a month as their father-son bonding activity. He knew his stuff, and her confidence grew with each idea and piece of advice.

But why was he helping her?

"Do you want to come and practice on our lane before doing it on your own? My dad won't mind," Chris offered. Was his dad that kind? If Chris was anything like him, then she believed it. But he was the guy who'd gotten a bj from two girls, and he'd set a fire at school. He couldn't be lovely.

"Yeah, maybe if my dad lets me," Lucie replied before ducking her head. How embarrassing that she had to ask her dad.

"Hey, Lucie." Emma swaggered up to them.

"Ems, thanks for earlier," Lucie said.

Emma shrugged. "He pissed me off when he tried to embarrass you in front of Jess's dad to make himself look better. Anyway, I took your go too. I got you a strike to rub it in when I bowl badly on my go. I want him to know that my bad performance is because of him. He sent me to find you. What are you doing with this guy again?"

Chris tensed beside her. "What's your problem with me?"

"I know stuff about you," Emma replied, squaring up

to him even though he was a foot taller.

"You don't know anything other than what some random told you. The way Lucie talks about you, I assumed you didn't judge, and yet that's all you've done when it comes to me. So ask me anything, and I will answer it, but let me save you some time by talking about the biggest rumours: I've never set any fires at school, I haven't slept with a teacher, and I haven't got any tattoos, although I will get one soon."

Emma glared back at him and folded her arms slowly. "Whatever. I still don't want you around my sister."

Lucie sucked in her breath.

"Why not?"

"Because… because she…"

"Because she what, Emma?" Lucie asked, finding an angrier voice than she'd ever used on her sister. Lucie stood between Chris and Emma and stared her down.

"I don't know," Emma replied with a shrug. "You're the hard-working one who doesn't get into trouble."

"Then trust that I know what I'm doing and that I won't get into trouble now. All we're doing is chatting," Lucie replied.

"Fine." Emma stood back, and Lucie turned to find Chris red-faced. Emma continued to scowl. "Don't hurt her, okay, or I'll get you."

"I promise not to set fire to her books or tattoo her thighs," he replied with a roll of his eyes. Lucie covered her mouth with her hand.

"Or get her to give you a bj in science." Emma smirked.

Chris's mouth dropped. "That one is still going around? Bloody hell. I should stop joking altogether."

Emma shrugged and turned to Lucie. "Do you want a

birthday glass of Coke? It will be fun to keep Dad waiting and piss him off a bit longer."

Chris gasped. It was lucky she liked his goofiness, or she'd have been hiding because of his dramatic reactions. "It's your birthday? Why didn't you say?" Chris asked.

"It's not until Sunday," she replied, shrugging to dismiss it. She hated birthdays, and this was going to be her eighteenth. Everyone else from school talked about how drunk they'd get on their birthdays and the parties they'd be having. As the eldest in the year, she should have set a wild example. They wouldn't be inviting her to their parties. Maybe she should ask Chris for ideas of what she could do in the holiday park to raise hell.

"This changes everything," he replied ominously, but the dimples returned. Heat swept over the back of Lucie's neck, and her palm was now so sweaty she nearly dropped the ball she was cradling. Why did everything get so hot when he smiled? She eyed him warily, but he didn't say anymore and continued to offer a massive grin.

Emma watched him too. Was she smiling now? "A diet Coke for me."

"Not this again," Emma replied, her smile quickly replaced with an eye-roll. She huffed before adding, "I'll be back in a sec with full-fat Cokes for both of us." She'd emphasised the words *full-fat*.

As she walked off, Chris asked, "What was that about?"

"I overheard some girls at school laughing about the way I looked so I was thinking I should lose some weight," she confessed, unsure why she was telling him.

"Seriously? But you're perfect," he whispered.

"Stop giving me these lines. You can't say something

like that when you don't know me," Lucie hit back. "Stop trying to make me like you by saying all these nice things about me."

Chris stared back, and he shoved his hands in his pockets. "I didn't realise that was what I was doing. Fine, maybe perfect was too much. But everything I've seen about you so far, I like, apart from when you believe what everyone tells you about me. I want to help your confidence, but maybe you don't want that from me."

She hid her surprise with a cough. Even though Chris confused her at times, he brought her joy. A pride beyond anything she'd felt in her life covered her body. It was like little lights that she'd never found a switch for began to light up one after another. It reminded Lucie of Christmas when she and Emma screwed each bulb on the old tree lights tighter to understand why none of them would light up. But halfway around, they found that one of the bulbs had broken, and when they changed the broken bulb, all the lights came alive in reds, blues, and greens. Finally, she found her confidence. It was like finding her broken bulb. Did he say he liked everything he'd seen about her so far? No one said that to her. Usually, she was too lanky, short, skinny, fat, and always too dull.

"Okay," she replied with a mouth so dry it came out as a rasp. What else did you say to that? "But I wish I had your confidence like all the time. I've never stood up to anyone else before."

He laughed, not cruelly, but what was the meaning behind the sound? "Do you think so? I can tell you the secret to my confidence."

She nodded with a half-smile.

"But not yet. How about you meet me tomorrow morning back at the beach around nine? It would be great to see you and, of course, get my drawing off you."

Was he holding his breath as he waited?

As she adjusted her grip on the ball that was threatening to slip from her sweaty hands, she spied her dad. He was storming her way, his face still blotchy but now red too.

She had to make her decision quick. She wanted to say yes, but what would that mean? Her dad was getting closer. Noisy arcade machines decorated with plastic palm trees shouted in the background as if adding a soundtrack to her panic. Emma was on her way back too, and she was glaring at their dad. A fight was brewing.

Chris's question hung in the air. Lucie's heart sped up, and her hands trembled. If they didn't meet tomorrow, they might never see each other again. Lucie took a breath and yanked her ponytail. Her heart thundered in her chest. She opened her mouth but still faltered.

"Is this where you've been all this time, talking to some boy? We've been waiting for you. It's not just rude to me but also Jessica's parents. Steve and Jacky have been very patient because you were supposed to be getting us all drinks, but this? Yet again, I'm ashamed of you," he ranted.

"Seriously?" Chris jumped in before Lucie could speak. "Because she was talking to someone? Are you for real?"

"This doesn't concern you, whoever you are. This conversation is between my unruly daughter and me. And you"—her dad was now pointing at Emma—"you were meant to bring her back. The pair of you are ruining this holiday with your silliness and impertinence."

"Chill out, mate," Chris said, bouncing on his feet. His laces were undone. Lucie focused on the trip hazard as a distraction from the confrontation.

"I am not your mate, and a punk like you doesn't get to disrespect me. Now leave my family alone." He dismissed him with a wave of his hand. Chris's jaw was hard and his nostrils flared as her dad turned to her and Emma. "Get back to the lane and apologise to your mother."

"No," Lucie replied, surprising herself. "You've been rude to my friend."

"Excuse me? You did not dare to answer me back," he snapped as he stood closer to Lucie, crowding her and forcing her to stand back.

Chris jumped in, his feet slapping against the plastic floor. "Leave her alone."

People were staring. Lucie winced as her face flamed hotter. The Stepford families were gawping, forcing her to dip her head, but she continued to see their judgement. Then, one by one, they turned their children away.

"It's fine," Lucie replied meekly as her mum walked towards them with a pale face.

"You're making a scene. Are you proud of yourself?" her dad asked, drawing more attention. "Everyone is looking at the silly little girl who throws a tantrum because she wants to talk to a boy."

Tears welled in her eyes as she walked back towards the lane, passing her mum, who whispered something at Emma. Lucie had tried to stand up to her dad, and it'd turned her into what he'd said—a silly little girl. Jess was mouthing something to her, but Lucie focused on Jess's disappointed parents, Steve and Jacky, who stood behind her. Everyone was embarrassed by her.

Chris wasn't a good friend for her, and her dad had made sure that Chris wouldn't want anything to do with her now anyway. Half a day around him, she was in trouble and hated herself more than usual.

CHAPTER TWELVE

PRESENT DAY

"Chris Jones?" Lucie asked, her mouth suddenly dry and her palms sweaty.

Chris jumped up and pulled her into a hug. He wasn't using Lynx Africa anymore, but there were familiar notes to his scent. Leather and citrus filled her lungs, and she repressed the impulse to sigh into his neck. His hair was a little shorter, and his body had filled out nicely. His navy suit clung to his muscles and displayed his physical change. She should be playing it cool, but it was as if her body already decided she needed comfort after a traumatic morning. It responded to the trust it once had in him, and she relaxed against his solid form. After all this time, she expected little or no internal reaction, but having him close sent a heat running through her body. Her limbs were like jelly, yet she vividly remembered every moment they spent together. Although his body was mostly muscle, Chris's cuddle was soft, and she closed her eyes, pushing the build-up of tension from her morning away. She sighed softly.

"I can't believe it's you," he whispered in her ear, causing a tingle to dance across of the back of her neck. Lucie had travelled the world before and after university and seen things that made her skin sparkle with excitement, but nothing she'd experienced in those months compared to this. He still had the power to make her shiver when he whispered. "You're blonde now, which suits you. Eight years older Lucie is even more beautiful than the one I spent the best weekend with. How is that?"

Heat radiated through her cheeks, and she let the hug go on a little longer to hide her body's reaction. But she didn't want to let go either.

"You look well," she stuttered, trying to get her voice back under control as his back muscles rippled against her lingering hand. She hadn't searched for him online for years. The idea of doom scrolling through photos of him with a stunning girlfriend or finding out he'd given up on his dreams was unnecessary. But now, as he stood in front of her, she regretted all the opportunities she could have taken to contact him. "And you scrub up well too."

Chris released her, and his eyes met hers. It was as if she hadn't seen him properly before the hug, and she nearly fell back at the change in him from eight years before. Her memories hadn't done him justice. Then, he was the most gorgeous guy she'd ever met, but now he was a man. The barest shadow of facial hair covered his chin, and his cheekbones were more defined. The bags under his eyes were a tiny bit bigger, but the dimples were still there when he smiled, and his sparkly green eyes floored her. Time had passed, and yet it was like they were in the forest on the beach, staring at each other as she drew him.

The rush from having him in front of her made her legs tremble. She took a deep breath as he spoke. "I know! I don't normally wear anything like today's suit. Thankfully I still had it in the back of my wardrobe from the last interview I wore it to. I still prefer jeans and a hoodie, but today is a special day," he replied with a massive smile.

Was he getting engaged? Maybe his baby was being blessed. She had so much to ask him, and there was more from that weekend that she needed to explain.

"You look smart too and that skirt matches the blue of your eyes. Did you have it made especially?"

"You're still the same Chris I remember," she replied, the corners of her mouth twitching with a smile. Teenage Chris would have asked that nonsense question too.

"Ha! I guess I am. Anyway, I have so much to tell you," he said, clapping his hands together with glee. It only took a glance, but there was no wedding ring on his finger. She released a breath, and the tension in her shoulders eased a little. "And so much I want to know. Are you free now?"

"Yes, for an hour," Lucie replied without hesitation.

"I'm free for an hour too. I got here early because I'm not allowed to be late today. This day is more important than anything—well, it is to the person I love the most," he said ominously, and his eyes twinkled. Her stomach bubbled quietly. Surely, she wasn't jealous? Chris was practically a stranger.

"Do you want to stay here?" Lucie asked, twisting her tired ankles. She was like the awkward teenager from when she first met Chris. Her skin tingled at his proximity. Would it be weird to stay for a drink in the place they had promised they'd meet before they broke each other's hearts? The memory of sitting in the booth, tears brimming her eyes as she willed him to walk through the door and remind her of her strengths, was heartbreaking. He never did walk through the door, and instead, she picked up her broken pieces herself. She'd learnt to be strong, to rely on herself, and to keep fighting. And yet now here he was. "Isn't there a pub near here called The Sidings Inn?"

Chris raised an eyebrow. "Isn't that place famous for being a perfect dumping spot? I'm sure I've had a couple of awkward dates there that never led to anything else. Are you going to dump me again?

"I'm joking, by the way," he said, his dimples showing. There was so much to talk about. "Let's see what it's like, Lucie Smith." He took her hand in his before she could say anything else. "I've heard they have the best ice cream sundaes."

*****

There was nothing fancy about the pub. It was the sort of place that people went at night to consume cheap drinks quickly before heading for a dance at an equally dodgy establishment. The smell of bacon and baked beans lingered from the all-day breakfasts. It combined with burnt coffee beans and pints of beer to bring a sick sensation to the tastebuds. Occasionally there was the tap from a cue hitting a ball in the corner. Some guys taking an early lunch break were making the most of the pool table while languishing over a pint. Songs played in the background. Lucie recognised the last bars of Green Day's "Wake Me Up When September Ends," but it quickly jumped into the Motown classic "You Can't Hurry Love" by The Supremes. It was an eclectic mix. Maybe there was a jukebox somewhere so you could pick your own tunes.

The pub was another addition to the city that made Lucie love Bristol. When she and Emma were younger, they'd get the bus to the city centre on Saturdays and attempt to find the gaudiest and cheapest keepsake. They'd had a lot of fun until they found the beauty beyond the city centre. All the different areas inspired their creativity, although it was street art that inspired Lucie while Emma loved the weekend markets. Bright patterned clothes, handmade jewellery, and beautifully designed trinkets that frequently came with stories made each neighbourhood special for different reasons.

Although there were quite a few people in the converted train shed pub, there was lots of space between the tables, and there was no danger of patrons overhearing their conversation. It was the perfect place to say a final goodbye to Bradley later. The low wooden beams and pillars every couple of metres made it appear cosy, especially with the shabby chic décor and soft lighting. In their dimly lit corner, it was as if they were in their own world, surrounded by memories and moments not yet spoken.

"I can't get over your hair," Chris said, his hand paused mid-air as if unsure about touching it. She'd filled him in briefly about her reasons for being in Bristol and was waiting to hear more about him. The blonde was a significant change, but she was pleased he liked it. It made her love it more.

"You can touch it if you want," she replied with a smile. Was it weird to offer that? He leant across the wooden table and fingered a couple of strands. Electricity zipped through her scalp before criss-crossing through her limbs. Was this the same for everyone who came face-to-face with their first love? It had to be that. She couldn't let herself believe it meant more.

CHAPTER THIRTEEN

"I propose a toast," Chris announced, his eyes sparkling and his grin never fading. Lucie shivered at his Bristolian lilt. He held his beer aloft. "To Lucie, her new hair, and the job she has to get because she is brilliant."

She held her wine glass in the air. She'd need some alcohol-induced courage to dump Bradley later. The music moved on again, and soft notes of "Everywhere" by Fleetwood Mac acted as the soundtrack to their celebrations.

"And to you too." She clinked her glass with his beer bottle. "Although I don't know why you're in this high-quality suit," she added. Imagine if he was on the way to get married. Her stomach churned. But the guy deserved to be happy, and who was she to him anyway? Too scared to ask, she attempted a different query to gain clues from his life. "Did you go into psychology?"

His laugh was deep and warm. Something about it filled Lucie's insides and made her belly flop. She hadn't felt anything like that in such a long time. How hadn't she realised that those emotions were missing from her life? It was like a rekindling of the innocence she'd felt when she'd been with him. She was jaded from online dating, and cracks appeared in her heart from years spent attempting to form adult relationships. It was impossible to protect herself from the hurt that hit regularly without forcing herself to shut down vulnerability and genuine emotions too.

"No, and you'll never guess why I'm wearing this. But first, you have to tell me about your dream job. Did you interview for a local law firm? I'm surprised your dad is letting you work anywhere but his place. Is it one of the big Bristol firms?" he asked enthusiastically. It was her turn to laugh. Everything had changed after that snapshot weekend together, yet her aching belly and the goose pimples on her arms reminded her she was a teenager when around him. "How cool would it be if you moved here? I would happily show you the best bars if you wanted."

But she wouldn't get to move to Bristol. Yesterday, Invo, the other place she'd interviewed at in Scotland, offered her a low-paid role on the lowest rung of the ladder, a position below the one she'd interviewed for. But it was money, and it was her last option, as her mum was leaving the country. Lucie's current home in a tiny village in the middle of nowhere was beautiful, but it wasn't the place for her anymore, especially now that her mum was selling the house. The countryside cottage may have been eighty miles away from the city she stood in now, but it was like another country. She'd never have another reason to come back here.

Her belly flopped again, and she fought to hide her smile. Suddenly her dream job was further from her grasp. There was too much at stake. Having the possibility of Chris back in her life was too much to contemplate. "I'm not going to get the job. I fluffed a crucial question. But if I'd gotten it, I would have loved to go to the best bars with you. I didn't interview at a law firm, though," she said it quietly as if proclaiming the truth would jinx her chances of getting the job even more. "I'm a graphic designer."

He paused, the rim of his beer bottle at his lips. At his raised eyebrows, she grinned wide. "You're kidding me? But the lawyer thing?"

Lucie shrugged, but she still had this need to share her vulnerabilities with him. "It wasn't easy to convince my dad to let me change career plans. But my mum was behind me every step of the way. Some stuff went on after that weekend, and I ended up travelling for a bit and studying at Brighton University." There was so much more she could tell him—about the drama with her dad and the reasons for it. Maybe she could broach how the "some stuff" after that weekend was partly why they'd never seen each other again. But Chris was a stranger, wasn't he?

Chris banged down his beer bottle, sending froth sloshing down the glass and onto the table. His smile was broad and his dimples deep enough for the tips of her fingers. "This is the best news ever. You went travelling?"

Lucie nodded. Few people would understand how significant that was. University friends had no idea how bereft of confidence she'd been at the age of seventeen. But Chris knew. They'd shared so much of who they were that weekend.

"I have a lot of questions."

"Then ask away. I know it sounds cheesy, but you inspired me." Lucie fought the temptation to cover her face. She nibbled at her lip as he looked over at her.

"Cheesy is good," he said with a smile before taking her hands in his. Her skin flushed with heat, and the memories of her shaky legs and tingling arms at seventeen came rushing back. "I may have made you think about things when we met, but you were the one who wanted to achieve something and then pushed yourself to do it. Your passion and hope were incredible, but they were a little hidden from the world."

She said softly, "You helped me find them and own them. You changed my life in all sorts of ways." She eased her hands out of his, and briefly, his mouth turned down. He hid it quickly with a smile, but his eyes didn't twinkle, and there were no dimples. Did he think she didn't want his touch? Lucie pushed up her sleeve to show him the tattoo she ran her thumb across when anxious. "Be the Exception" was written in italics across her wrist. "You helped me be the exception, and I'm grateful for that."

Chris placed a hand on his heart and sighed. His action drew her attention to his tie, which had little white hearts scattered all over it. She smiled. The confidence he'd helped her find was still there. Would many other twenty-six-year-old men wear hearts on their tie without trying to pass it off as a joke? She quickly reviewed the guys she'd dated over the last year. None of them would have worn it, unless ironically, and if they had worn it ironically, they would have mentioned it within the first five minutes of meeting. Bradley wore braces because he'd seen them in articles from London Fashion Week, and all his hipster friends wore them. He hated missing out on clothing trends. He'd proudly told her about the boiler suit he once wore to a wedding. Why did she date him for so long?

Maybe Chris was going somewhere romantic. Disappointment threaded through her, and the marks across her heart throbbed. She shook her head. It was okay if he'd found his "the one." He was her first love, but she couldn't expect it to be the same for him. She didn't wait for him, so why wouldn't he be in a relationship? Every moment she spent with him reminded her he was someone special. He deserved happiness. Whoever he was with was lucky.

"I can't believe you got that phrase as a tattoo. That is so cool," Chris followed up before Lucie had the opportunity to regret showing him her inking. "I have to show you something."

He eased his suit jacket off his shoulders and rolled up a sleeve, revealing a muscular forearm. Women were always swooning over men with strong forearms in the rugby romances she read, but none of the heroes in those stories had anything on Chris. Dark hairs covered his tanned skin. It was another reminder that he'd become a man since their time together. Lucie's stomach clenched as she studied every inch, from the lines in his hands to the veins that threaded up his forearms. She got a glance before he held up the back of his arm, but she committed every glimpse of his skin to memory.

"See," he said, pointing out his tattoo. On the back of his forearm, below his elbow, was an intricate star. It was made up of swirls and surrounded by shading as if it was flying.

Lucie's gasp was so loud that strangers from a nearby table looked over. It was her star.

"How do you have that star? I drew that. Didn't I?" she whispered. The strangers continued their chatter.

"You added it to your drawing of me. You showed me the Saturday we spent together. The tattoo artist copied it. He told me that it was one of the most beautiful and artistic stars he'd ever seen, and he'd tattooed a lot of them."

"I considered designing tattoos, but I didn't think

they'd look as good in reality. The person who did this was a true artist," she replied, fascinated by the inking in front of her. It was a carbon copy of her drawing. Her hand hovered near Chris's tattoo. It was as if he understood her unspoken request to touch it when he nodded. Slowly she traced the image. "Hold on. I put the piece of paper with the star drawing on it in the bin, near that café. How did you get it?"

"I took it back out when you'd gone and kept it." He rolled his sleeve back down and reached for his wallet. She missed touching his skin already. It was smooth and soft. He pulled a worn piece of A4 paper out of his tired leather wallet. He unfolded the paper, slowly revealing the jagged edge from where she'd ripped it out the pad. The creases in the folds caught her eye as he slid it across to her. There were other lighter creases too, from where she'd scrunched it up and chucked it in the bin at the holiday park. The memory was vivid. She recalled the worn red bin next to the coffee shop and the shame she'd been filled with when she binned it before running away. She'd revisited the pain of that moment several times over the last eight years. The shame had gone. If she had stayed and dealt with what had happened, how different would her life have been?

"Do you remember why you drew that particular image and our time that afternoon?" he asked gently, his deep voice cutting through her thoughts.

Her ears were burning with embarrassment. Why didn't Chris ask her what he wanted to know? His question was about her anxiety. She needed to tell him what had changed. Lucie gulped a mouthful of wine, desperate to prevent the dryness clogging her throat. The wine was ice cold, and it froze her gullet.

Was it finally the time to tell him what happened that weekend?

Chapter Fourteen
Eight Years Earlier, Saturday

It had rained throughout the night, a deluge her mum commented on when Lucie found her staring out the French window at seven that morning. Lucie was always up early, although usually to study before school. She kept the routine throughout the school holidays too. But, that morning, as Lucie watched the downpour, with her pink fleece dressing gown wrapped tightly around her and a cup of tea in her hand, she admitted to herself that studying was the last thing on her mind. Her belly was a mixture of churning guilt interspersed with tiny butterflies sneaking in to tell her that she liked Chris. Since dawn, she'd lain awake, remembering every word from the bowling alley.

Last night after the incident, Lucie's dad made her mum escort her back to the lodge to "reflect on her actions and choices" but not before forbidding her from seeing Chris again. Normally she would have accepted the decision and avoided Chris at all costs, but the butterflies told her to defy her dad and go. He wouldn't find out. But even if Chris was attracted to her or wanted to be her friend, he wouldn't be at the beach because she'd treated him so badly at the bowling alley.

Lucie checked her watch before staring in the mirror.

She could walk near the beach around nine, and if he wasn't there, she'd be okay with that. Her dad wouldn't be up for ages based on the alcohol fumes that had wafted through the lodge when Lucie fetched a glass of water in the night.

What if Chris was at the beach and didn't want to speak to her? She had to give it a chance. But that led to more questions. Should she put a lot of make-up on or be more natural? It wasn't a date, and she didn't have any make-up anyway. How could she make an effort without looking like she hadn't bothered? She could go into Emma's room to get her opinion on her planned outfit, but then Jess and Emma would continue the Chris being trouble stories again, and Emma would stop Lucie from going. Last night she'd grumbled about how he was the reason their dad had shouted at them and how the drama wouldn't have happened if not for him. It was out of character for her not to side with Lucie, but then even Emma had moments of behaving in order to keep from pushing their dad too far. No one in the family liked it when he started shouting.

Lucie glimpsed at her watch again. It was 8:30 now. What if her dad surprised everyone and got up? If she were early, it wouldn't matter if Chris came or not because she'd be there. The butterflies fluttered harder as she grabbed her bag and slipped out the front door. Was this the most rebellious thing she'd ever done? As she ran down the road from the lodge, she was sure eyes were on her back. Every step took her farther away from the safety of her dull life and closer to danger. Her fingers tingled with excitement while her belly told her she was about to throw up. The voices in her head were ramping up her anxiety, reminding her of the trouble she would be in if her dad found out where she'd gone.

Her feet thudded the ground as she sped up. It was the only sound in the forest and wasn't drowning out the anxiety that clung to every part of her brain.

"Shut up. Shut the hell up." Her shouts echoed through the forest. Usually, she was happy to be alone, but not when her thoughts spiralled. She eased her earphones into her ears as a mum in black leggings and a loose jumper hopped into her path. Leggings and baggy jumpers made up the day uniform of the skinny jeans–wearing Stepford wives.

Lucie dodged her and ran faster as "Black and White Town" by The Doves filled her ears. Maybe that woman had been at the beach yesterday and at the bowling alley last night. She probably thought Lucie was crazy, but at least she didn't think she was boring. Unexpected giggles sprang free. People at the holiday park probably didn't consider her boring.

Am I a rebel?

She laughed harder as she ran faster. Within minutes, the beach came into view.

Lucie bounded onto the nearly empty beach and kicked off her shoes. It was 8:50. She spied the same gang of teenagers out of the corner of her eye. They were queuing for the inflatable assault course. No matter where she went, they were always there. Did they think she was a rebel or just rude? The girl from the day before caught her eye and raised her eyebrow. Lucie picked up her shoes and stepped closer to the water, creating more space between them.

Maybe if she closed her eyes, they'd stay away from her.

She dropped her bag and shut her eyes. What if they came to attack her? Now she wouldn't know.

Stop being silly. They don't care about you.

The wet sand clumping under the bridge of her feet distracted her overthinking brain. She filled her lungs with the clear air and slowly breathed it out. The night rain resembled a shower that fell after a series of sweltering days and cleared the heaviness from the atmosphere. It was like a fresh chapter. Lucie faced the water and pulled her earphones out to listen to the water lapping slowly on the beach, clearing the sand of yesterday. She opened one eye and checked if the teenagers had moved, but they were still in the queue, shoving each other and laughing. Cool air covered her skin, and she closed her eye again to stop distracting herself from the atmosphere. The scent of fir trees filled her lungs, and goose pimples dotted her arms. But she wasn't cold. For the first time in a long time, she had hope. But hope for what?

What if Chris turned up? What would she say to him? Maybe he'd want to shout at her as her dad had. Her thoughts were jumbled, yet her skin itched with excitement, and energy filled her limbs even though she'd barely slept the night before.

Suddenly the smell of Lynx Africa replaced the scent of fir. Chris was here. It made her want to laugh, but why? Lucie didn't open her eyes. What if he wasn't as attractive as she'd thought and she'd built it up too much in her head? It would serve her right for being so superficial. She hated it when people judged her looks, so why was she doing it to someone else? Other worries compounded like the sand beneath her feet. What if he was angry? Or what if she blushed and Chris laughed at her? He stood close but not close enough for their arms to touch. He didn't speak. She squeezed her eyes tight, willing him to say something, yet terrified of what that something might be.

A couple of voices carried on the breeze from the pancake house. Families were laughing about the smiley faces they'd found on their pancakes after a chef got creative with the chocolate chips. A child was probably sitting on the decking outside the pancake house, based on the direction of the sound. They asked someone what the moon looked like and if stars had feelings.

Could your soul smile? A rush of something like joy filled her heart, and a smile rested on her lips. If Chris were angry, he wouldn't have come, or he'd have said something, right? She breathed in his spicy deodorant again and sighed.

"Do they?" Chris whispered in her ear. It made her goose bumps multiply like little viruses all over her skin. It was as if she was seven again, and her best friend had told her that when boys tagged you in a game of chase, they gave you the lurgy. Did Chris give her the lurgy? Her brain stopped working when he stood this close, and sweat beaded the back of her neck under her ponytail. Maybe this was what love did to you.

You're not in love. Don't be silly. You've only just met.

She cleared her mind and immersed herself in the moment. "Do they what?" she whispered back, her eyes closed and her body facing the water.

"Do stars have feelings?" At his voice, the hairs on her neck stood on end.

Could she hear his smile through his words?

"There's one way to find out. We should spread our wings and reach for them." Why did she say that? It was the sort of thing that girls at school would laugh at her for.

It wasn't logical or something that a grown-up would say, yet she said it to Chris. There was something about being around him that made her silly. It wasn't love—they were like primary school friends—but she couldn't explain the attraction on top of that.

"Okay, I'm spreading my arms now, but you have to as well." A balminess spread through her belly at the Bristolian lilt of his voice. She should have had that accent too, but her dad had made her practice clear-cut speech as a child. It made her love Chris's voice even more.

She opened her arms and brushed against him. Chris's skin was warm against hers. She tingled at the contact. They must have looked ridiculous.

Chris whispered again, "Now, what do we do? Do we ask the stars if they have feelings?"

"No." She smiled. She didn't know why she said the next thing. Was it hope that filled her heart or something more? "Now, we will change the world."

He didn't laugh or tell her she was an idiot. Instead, he said, "Spread your wings, reach for the stars, and you will change the world. Okay, I will."

Then he did something that made her breath catch and her heart stop. He entwined her fingers with his and held her hand. They stood together. Her hand was clammy, and his flesh was warm, but she refused to break contact. A guy had never held her hand before. Her heart went from stopping to beating rapidly. It was a bit like when she had an anxiety attack, but pleasant, although she was fighting to keep her trembling arms still. Even though she wore a ponytail and there was a freshness in the air, strands of her hair stuck to her sweaty neck. Happiness replaced a concern that she might ruin everything by existing.

"We can't stand here all day," she said after what could have been thirty seconds or ten minutes. Time had no distinguishable pattern when she was with him. She wanted to stay there all day, but she didn't want him to get awkward and suddenly pull his hands away. By doing it first, she'd stopped him rejecting her. Not that she was ditching him. But it was good to save face, right?

"It's a shame, but I suppose if we're going to change the world, we need to move," Chris replied without inflexion. "And I was hoping we'd play adventure golf this morning too."

A giggle fell from her lips. She opened one eyelid and gave him a side-eye. Lucie was blessed with him smiling at her, his dimples shadows in the sunshine.

"Okay, let's go," she said. Chris twisted his hand so they were no longer intertwined but linked. She forced out a breath at the realisation that he still wanted to hold her hand and reached for her rucksack. He didn't let go as she leaned down. Was this a weird game or joke he was playing on her? Hand in hand, they walked to the adventure golf and teased each other about who would be the ultimate champion. But what if her dad caught them? Lucie yanked at her ponytail.

CHAPTER FIFTEEN

They'd been playing adventure golf for half an hour, but progress had been slow due to the number of people who'd had the same idea as them.

"You seem to be struggling on that hole a bit," Lucie called out.

"Are you taking the piss?" Chris called back. The sun streamed through the trees and into her eyes.

"I was offering to help," she replied, stepping closer and bending while holding her putter out. "You need to hold your putter like this."

"No way. Shouldn't I be doing this?" he said, pretending to pole dance with his stick.

"Never mind," Lucie huffed with a roll of her eyes. There was an awkwardness between them that hadn't been there when they'd chatted at the beach.

"You don't like my dancing?" he asked as he turned so he wasn't facing her. He reversed towards her while bouncing his bum. "I'm twerking."

"You're what?"

"Twerking. It was on YouTube," he said as his bum got closer. "It's making you smile. I know it is."

Lucie held onto her smile as hard as possible, twisting her mouth into a variety of shapes to prevent it from appearing. "Nope, no smile here."

"Not even when I do this?" He spanked his bum as it bounced. He gave her a quick wink over his shoulder.

It was too much. The coolest guy she'd met was "twerking" and spanking his arse to make her smile. Laughter bubbled in her throat, bursting out before she quickly covered her mouth.

"I made you laugh," he said, holding the putter above his head in triumph. "I win!"

"Fine," she replied, rolling her eyes but unable to push down the corners of her mouth into anything less than a grin. "I'm still beating you, though."

"True." He furrowed his brow and rubbed his chin dramatically. "I'd best get this ball in then."

He squatted down as if he was in a professional golf tournament and not trying to putt a ball between two giant plastic toadstools. "Hmmm," he murmured, popping a finger to his lips in an exaggerated manner. "What to do? What to do?"

He stood again and bent over. His baseball shirt rode up and revealed his back above the waistband of his shorts. His skin was a little tanned and unblemished.

Stop staring. But heat filled her cheeks before covering her body like a blanket as she gawked.

"Am I annoying you yet?" he asked without turning.

"No." The one-syllable word came out strangled.

Chris turned, and his brow furrowed. "You okay?"

"Yep. I think I swallowed a fly," Lucie lied as she pretended to swat non-existent flies around her. "Can't get away from them here."

He shrugged before returning to his shot and smacking the ball way too hard for the two metres it needed to cover. It flew off the little patch of green and landed in the bush.

They continued to be stuck even when they found the ball, got back to the green, and putt it. Families surrounded them, either waiting for them to finish each hole or delaying them from getting to the next as small children tried to putt the ball. One little girl picked up the ball and dropped it in the hole while her parents were busy with her baby brother.

"I got a one hole," she shouted proudly.

"Well done, darling," the dad shouted back, his attention on the baby decked out in blue bawling from the pram as an exhausted mum cooed over them.

"We're going to be here a while," Lucie whispered, breaking the silence.

"Let's talk about last night then," Chris replied with a blank face. "I wasn't sure if you'd be here today. You were kinda rude to me at the bowling alley."

She rounded on him. "I was rude? Me? You got me in trouble when you spoke to my dad the way you did."

"I was defending you," he said with a huff. "No one else was on your side."

"I don't need anyone on my side," she grunted.

"He shouted at me in front of my dad after you left," Chris said, a sadness laced through his words. "He told me that I shouldn't come anywhere near you again, or he'd make trouble for my dad and me and get us thrown out of this place."

"Are you serious?" Lucy sat on the edge of one of the logs near the next hole. The baby was quietening down now, but the family still hadn't got their balls in the hole. "I'm so sorry. I didn't know. I haven't seen him since Mum took me back to the lodge. Why did you meet me if he said that?"

"Don't you believe me?" Chris's brows furrowed.

"No, I do. But I mean, why would you risk seeing me? It could ruin your holiday."

He shrugged. "I dunno. I like hanging out with you. You make me laugh, and you say some random things and…"

"And?" Was he going to say he fancied her?

"And I can be myself. Like, I don't need to do anything crazy, and you'll still smile and listen to me. We're both a bit different."

He didn't fancy her then. She was like a friend to him. She hid her face in case he read her thoughts. "True. You don't need to impress me. I know it's not how I seem, but I don't care if away from here you're a bad boy or Mr. Perfect."

"Seriously? You don't care if I'm popular or anything? Like I can be whoever I want?"

"Sure," she replied. How did she sound like the confident one all of a sudden? "It's not like we'll see each other again after this weekend. I'm surprised you came today."

If he was disappointed by what she said, there were no signs of it. Lucie fixed her smile to hide the sadness.

"I didn't think you'd be here either. I laughed when I saw you on the beach. You were so calm compared to when you were standing up to your dad."

"I barely stood up to him," she said dismissively.

He shrugged. "More than you have before."

"Yeah," she conceded quickly with a smile. "I guess I've got to start somewhere."

He grinned back at her. "Totally."

A gruff voice caught her attention. "Kathleen, I don't want to play this. My head hurts, and it's a game for children."

"Shit, that's my dad," she whispered, dragging Chris behind a tree.

"This isn't how you stand up to him," he replied softly as they stood close but not quite touching. He took a deep breath as Lucie looked up into his eyes. His face was a little red. The scent of Lynx was making her dizzy, and her heart beat faster. "But maybe you can do that another time."

Lucie's head was swimming, and as she wobbled, Chris grabbed her by the waist. "Just to steady you if that's okay?"

"Yeah, thanks," she replied. His hand was hot through her T-shirt. "How long should we stay here?"

Her dad's voice was louder now. Chris leaned down and whispered in her ear, "A little longer." Goose pimples appeared on her arms, but she wasn't cold. Instead, her whole body was burning up.

His green eyes lingered on her lips, and she licked them. Should she be wearing lip gloss like the girls at school did? She'd swiped a bit of Vaseline on her lips that morning as she left, but that was to stop them from cracking in the heat. Vaseline wasn't sexy, and it had worn off anyway.

Her tongue stuck to the roof of her mouth. They were so close now that Chris's heartbeat thudded against her chest.

"I was thinking—"

"Excuse me, you can't take the putters away," a pimply-faced teenager in a green T-shirt bearing the holiday park's logo said, suddenly beside them. "If you want to finish the game, then you need to finish the round."

Chris jumped away from her and rubbed the back of his neck as Lucie stepped as far away as possible while still hiding from her parents. She peeked behind the tree. Her dad was closer now and still moaning about his head and the heat. "I think we've finished."

Chris's brow furrowed, but he shrugged and grabbed Lucie's putter, quickly handing them back to the guy.

"Where are your balls?" he said as he puffed up his chest, which drew their attention to his slight frame.

"No idea, mate. I can't seem to find them either," Chris said with a sigh.

"Let's go this way, or Dad will see us," Lucie whispered as she grabbed his hand, and they legged it through the trees.

CHAPTER SIXTEEN

Sweet smells wafted around Lucie and Chris. It brought back memories of Saturday mornings with Emma and her mum when Dad was sleeping off an evening of "difficult work." That was what their mum said, although it was only as a teenager that she realised he hadn't been tired but hungover from schmoozing clients. Their mum would fill them with pancakes and then take them to city centre on the bus to give their dad peace. Even though they had to eat quietly, they had fun. One of their favourite games was silent karaoke, where one of them mouthed a popular song while the others guessed it. The silent disco was fun too, until their dad shouted at them for shuffling too loudly.

Lucie's mum made all their mornings fun, taking them around the city to the big local clock where a little statue hit a bell on the hour and to the river to feed the birds. Although there were never any birds, Emma would eat all the bread and then pretend to be a duck and quack around the park to make them laugh.

But I'm turning into an adult now. Those days are gone. Although she asked Emma nicely enough, she'd probably repeat her duck impression and make Lucie smile.

Chris, who was air drumming with his knife and fork, smiled back at her. He'd probably make a duck impression too, if she asked. He didn't care how people looked at him.

He lifted his head suddenly. "Are you smiling at my awesome drumming? I am brilliant. I have air drumming trophies. I'd show you, but you'd probably tell me you couldn't see them. The trophies are made of air too."

She rolled her eyes, but her lips squeezed into a smile, much to her annoyance.

"Very funny. Although I'd love to 'see' these imaginary trophies," Lucie said before tipping her head to the side and giving a pouting grin.

"Woah, who said they're imaginary?" he replied with a cheeky smile.

Lucie sighed loudly and shook her head. "I was smiling because I can't believe I beat you at adventure golf. Well, I would have beaten you if we'd finished. I was winning," she said as they sat at the pancake house. The loser paid for pancakes, but she wasn't going to hold him to it; she had money. "I'm rubbish at all sports."

"Three positives," he replied, quickly stopping her in her stride. His hair had more gel in than the day before. He'd pushed up the sleeves of his baseball shirt. It fitted him well, as the bending and stretching at adventure golf proved. A blush returned to her cheeks when she remembered the skin of his back again. What would his chest be like? Would it ripple as she'd seen on guys on television, or would it resemble a footballer's, flat and smooth?

She took a deep breath.

"I'm good at art, I wear a great ponytail, and I was beating you at adventure golf?" Her voice went up at the end, and she pulled on her earlobe briefly. Her dad often pointed out that it was another one of her nervous ticks. Had he said it to make her stop or make her more nervous?

"Are you asking me or telling me?" Chris replied with a smile.

"How do you do that?" she asked. A blond waiter, around Chris's age or a bit older, plopped their pancakes down. With his bright blue eyes and perfect cheekbones, he could have been a YouTube star. If she'd bumped into him a week ago, Lucie would have crushed on him and daydreamed their first conversation, where he'd declare how much he fancied her. But with Chris in front of her, his green eyes sparkling with warmth, she only wanted him or to be around him.

"How do I do what?" he asked, his knife and fork clanging together as he ripped into his pancake.

Lucie paused to rest her serviette on her lap. She smoothed it across her shorts to avoid ruining them with a spillage. "How do you manage to be so confident all the time? You asked for a chocolate chip face pancake, but they're for kids. You weren't embarrassed."

He held a lump of the pancake smothered with the melted chocolate chips to his lips. Chocolate dripped down into the pool of melted ice cream on his plate. "If I don't ask for one, then I won't get it, and I wanted a smile on my pancake. Did you want one with chocolate chips on top too?"

She did, but she was too self-conscious to admit it. Instead, she yanked on her ponytail. She was more embarrassed that she hadn't had the confidence to ask for it. Slowly she cut her pancake into bite-sized pieces while contemplating Chris's words. A lump of banana squidged out from the pancake, and she chased it around the edge of the plate with her fork. Chris's choice of chocolate chips and vanilla ice cream looked yummier. Why did she choose the healthiest option on the menu?

"Can I let you into a secret about my confidence?" he asked quietly, leaning forward.

Lucie nodded keenly before dragging her chair closer to the table so she wasn't straining to hear him. It made a scraping noise on the floor. At the sound, she looked down and raised her shoulders as if to hide her face.

Chris continued, oblivious, "If I pretend to be confident, then people believe I'm confident. So, therefore, I am confident." He grinned before shoving another lump of pancake into his mouth.

"You're telling me that to be confident, all I need to do is act it? That's your big secret?" It couldn't be that simple. Chris must have another explanation for his self-assurance. Maybe this was a game, and she had to work out what was real and what wasn't. But as she gazed at him, he shrugged. That was it? She'd furrowed her forehead so tightly that she was in danger of giving herself a headache.

Lucie sighed and shook her head to get rid of the tightness before popping a piece of banana-filled pancake into her mouth.

He shrugged. "Yep, that's all you need to do. Act confident, and then people believe you're confident, and they haven't got anything to prove otherwise."

But it couldn't be that simple. She couldn't imitate it and then get away with people believing it. But Chris had appeared so sure of himself since the moment Lucie met him.

"You've finished your drink," Chris said, pointing at her glass with his knife. "I dare you to ask the waiter for a refill and then ask for some chocolate chips to go on your pancake because you want to make a smiley face."

"But won't that annoy him because I didn't ask for it

for the first time? Also, what if he's not allowed to do that? Or he might ask me to leave for being rude." How embarrassing would it be to get thrown out of the holiday village pancake house? And what if her parents were passing and they saw her?

"Lucie, chill out and stop overthinking everything. What if he says yes, or even no, and he never thinks about it again because it's no big deal?" Lucie bristled at his comments. Maybe he sensed it because Chris continued softly, "It isn't a big deal. Imagine what a confident person would do and then fake it like they're probably doing. He's coming over now."

Lucie's fingers trembled as she stared down at her pancake, now cut into perfect squares. She wouldn't be able to put a symmetrical smiley face on it anyway. She hid her shaking fingers under the table, but that made it tricky to tug on her ponytail.

"Is everything okay with your meals?" the waiter asked.

Was it harder to be confident around the waiter because he was attractive? No, that was a silly excuse. She simply wasn't a confident person. Both Chris and the waiter stared at her, waiting for her answer. Her face was boiling, and she fisted her hands in an attempt to stop the trembling. It was like the words were desperate to come out of her mouth, and if she didn't ask, then they would burn themselves on her tongue, reminding her for the rest of the day she was too gutless to say them. Her stomach churned. Why would Chris do this to her?

Lucie shook herself.

"Chocolate chips," she blurted out. The waiter frowned. Lucie winced. "Can I have some chocolate chips, please? I want to make a smiley face on my pancake."

"Sure," the guy said. "And do you want a refill of juice too? Your face is really red. It's like you've been climbing Everest or something."

"Yeah," she squeaked, fighting the urge to hide her face. "Juice too, please."

The waiter walked away. Occasionally he raised his eyebrow at her over his shoulder. It was as if he was trying to spy on the two-headed monster. But Chris's giddiness distracted her from the waiter.

Chris grinned and bounced on the vinyl bench. "You did it! You're amazing. I'm so proud of you."

The waiter had made it clear she was already bright red, but her face got even hotter.

"And every time you do something like that, it will get easier so that one day you won't think twice or get embarrassed." His joy was contagious.

Lucie's face cooled, and she smiled back. Chris was right. She'd done it, and nothing awful had happened even though she'd made an arse of herself. The adrenaline rush eased, and a fusion of elation and pride replaced it. Requesting the chocolate chips was terrifying, but it beat the shame that typically stayed with her throughout the day when she didn't ask for something or when she didn't speak up.

She sighed happily at Chris, who continued to fill his grinning gob with lumps of congealed chocolate and ice cream smothered pancake. She couldn't keep up with the emotions running through her when he was around.

Lucie stared out of the window, taking in the view. Families continued to play and get on with their lives, but she'd faced one of her fears.

"I really did it," she whispered.

Suddenly she caught a glimpse of her parents walking around the edge of the beach. Her mum's head was down, and she was wringing her hands together. Meanwhile, her dad gesticulated wildly. Even from a distance, she could see he was gnashing his teeth about something.

"What is he moaning about now?" Lucie hadn't realised she'd said it aloud until Chris gazed to where she was staring.

"I can't tell if he's having a go about something to your mum or at your mum. Is he angry a lot?"

"Not a lot, but it does happen. My mum manages him so that his temper is under control," Lucie replied with a sigh. Her mum's steps slowed, but her dad was focused on his rant. Usually, she and Emma spent six weeks with their mum's parents, Grandpa Jim and Grandma Callie, during the school holidays. But this year, their grandparents had asked for a summer without Lucie and Emma visiting so that they could go on a dream cruise around the world. She and Emma were too old to stay with them every summer anyway. The anecdote-filled postcards sent from a series of beautiful beach locations left a sad smile on her mum's face. "But he kicks off more these days."

Was that true, or was she noticing it more? Being home throughout the school holidays had opened her eyes to the behaviour she wasn't aware of due to having her head buried in books or attending after-school activities to help her university application. It wasn't that her dad shouted a lot, but the house changed when he was home. Messes were tidied quicker, and there was less laughter and silliness. When he was around, there was an atmosphere that Lucie sensed as soon as she walked through the front door. Occasionally she heard her mum crying when she thought everyone was out. Why was she with her dad if she was this unhappy? Maybe that was what love was. Was that why Lucie didn't argue with her dad about studying law? Because she loved him?

"Your mum looks sad." Chris stared out the window.

With each step her parents took, the gap widened between them until her mum was a couple of metres behind her dad. Suddenly he turned and shouted. Maybe Lucie was reading it wrong, but based on how he was throwing his hands in the air rather than pointing them in her direction, he wasn't angry with her. Even so, she was taking the brunt of his frustration. Maybe Emma had done something to upset him, or he'd seen Lucie and Chris at the adventure golf after all. Fear filled her belly. If that were true, she'd be in trouble when she got back to the lodge. Should she help her mum? But what if he yelled at Lucie too?

Lucie scrunched her serviette before tearing it into pieces. How could she leave her mum to her dad's moods, especially if it was her fault? Tears brimmed in Lucie's eyes. As a child, her mum tried to protect her and Emma from witnessing their dad being difficult, but now that she was nearly an adult, Lucie couldn't hide or pretend anymore. Her mum hadn't shown a genuine smile in a long time. Instead, she appeared to tolerate his digs and grumpiness as if she'd resigned herself to her future.

"Yeah, she does look sad. I thought growing up meant you made your own choices and had fun without limits, but it's like you can see more of the truth that's always been front of you." Maybe Lucie could help her like Emma helped Lucie. She hesitated and pulled her bottom lip through the slight gap between her teeth. Lucie dropped her head so that she could hide her tears from Chris.

"Lucie, don't feel bad. It happens to all of us at some point. I hate that I see the world differently the older I get. When I was younger, I was desperate to be an adult and live by myself. I believed it would all be midnight feasts and drinking as much cherryade as I wanted."

"How young were you when you thought this?"

"Last year, when I filled in my university application," he joked. "I am going to drink so much cherryade if I go to university."

His grin was disarming, but it didn't stop her from picking up on the word "if."

Before she had the opportunity to ask him what he meant, he continued, "You can't fix your parents, but you can live your life. So don't let them decide who you're going to be.

Lucie's mum appeared despondent even at a distance. "I should go and see her," Lucie announced although she stood gingerly. "I'll be back in a second."

Lucie darted out of the pancake house. What was she going to say anyway?

She stepped closer to her parents. *You can be the exception.*

"Look who it is," her dad grumbled when he glanced her way. "You rushed out this morning. I bet you were embarrassed by last night's tantrum."

"No, I—"

"I hope it wasn't to see that boy you were talking to in the bowling alley," he said, with the ranting tone he'd been using on her mum.

"So what if it was?" Lucie squealed, surprised at her words. She fought the temptation to turn and find Chris through the window of the pancake house. He didn't need to be dragged into her family dramas.

"Excuse me? I don't like your attitude. He's rubbing off on you, although I bet he's finding it very entertaining," her dad replied with a sneer. Her mum tried to interject, but he waved her away.

"What do you mean?" She yanked at her ponytail.

"There are two reasons why boys like that talk to girls like you." He rolled his shoulders as if he was already bored with the conversation. "He's either trying to use you, or he wants to humiliate you. Either way, you need to stay away from him for your future."

Was he right? She didn't have any experience to compare it to. And what did he mean by use her? She hid her gasp. Did he mean..? Surely not that.

"He's just being a friend," she mumbled.

Her mum finally interjected. "Of course he is. You're our good girl. He probably sees you like a little sister or like a holiday buddy. And I'm sure he isn't trying to humiliate you. He's probably bored because his girlfriend dumped him, and there wasn't anything else for him to do. That's what Emma said this morning."

Her father laughed loudly. Somehow he'd won points off the conversation without giving the final blow. "What?" he asked as her mum nudged him. "She knows she's not the sort of girl that guys like to spend time with. Her lack of boyfriends and friends proves that."

Tears welled in her eyes. Chris was chatting to her because she was one step up from boredom, and all her family knew it. Emma didn't say cruel things. She was the best sister there was, so she had to be correct.

Suddenly her dad's smile transformed as he glanced over her shoulder. He usually smiled like that when he was with clients. Lucie turned to find Jess's parents walking towards them. "Guys, where have you been? You've missed all the fun. Obviously, I beat Kathleen at golf. She tried but was no match for me. Steve, let me tell you how I got a hole in one."

Jess's parents joined them, and Lucie was quickly forgotten as they walked off in the direction of the activity centre.

She couldn't go back to the pancake house and face Chris now, but she couldn't leave him to face the bill either. She dropped her head but refused to sob in front of the Stepford wives huffing as they stepped awkwardly around her. She dug the heels of her hands into her closed eyes and held back tears.

A hand brushed her shoulder, and she flinched away.

"Lucie, are you okay?" Chris asked, his voice gentle. "Whatever he said to you can't be true."

"What did you hear?" she asked brusquely. She didn't need anyone else laughing at her.

"I didn't hear anything, but I saw you. You practically folded up when your parents spoke to you. Why? What did they say?" Chris's green eyes fixed on hers. If she hadn't known better, she would have said Chris cared, but that was impossible based on what her parents and Emma said, and everyone knew it.

"Nothing," she replied sullenly, but he continued to inspect her face. "I'd best go and pay. Don't worry. I was still going to pay. I know you don't have much money." Jess had mentioned something about that.

His face changed at her comment. "I wasn't worried. I have money. I've paid for our pancakes, and I got the rest of yours to go." He pushed the wrapped-up pancake in her direction. "I put the smiley face on for you but it didn't really work because you'd already cut it up so I tried doing lots of tiny smiley faces."

"Oh, right." She snatched the pancake. "Thanks."

"I had a plan for what we could do next, but I'm not sure you want to be around me, and that's okay. I'm not sure I want to be around you at the moment when you're lying and judging me. Maybe you will be good at law after all, Lucie, as you seem to be like your dad in some ways," Chris snapped before walking away.

"I don't lie! How dare you say I lie," she shouted, running after him. Her heart beat rapidly as she grabbed his arm and yanked him back to face her. "And I am nothing like him. Don't ever say that."

"Then stop judging me and stop judging yourself. You stood up to your dad, which was really impressive, and then he got in your head, and you're letting it ruin your day."

"Fine," she barked. "Let's not let him ruin it. Let's get out into the forest and do something crazy."

"Are you sure?" he asked cautiously, although one corner of his mouth kept bobbing as if he wanted to risk a smile.

"Yeah. I'm fed up with all these people who look the same and act the same, and yet I bet they have their own sordid secrets that they hide in their postcard-perfect lives." She unwrapped the leftovers of her pancake and snatched bites in anger. Chocolatey gooeyness filled her mouth as she thought of the things she'd believed about her own family in the past.

"Tell me about it. Right, come with me," Chris replied, encouraging her to walk beside him.

CHAPTER SEVENTEEN

The sun beat down on them as they cycled around the quieter paths of the forest. The park was popular for cyclists, and the lush greenery on either side of her was why. Thank goodness her mum insisted on renting bikes for the weekend. As she rode, a light breeze tickled her skin.

"I can't remember when I last rode a bike," she said as Chris coasted next to her. He was a bit gangly for his bike, and he'd nearly flown off the handlebars a couple of times.

"I haven't since I was fifteen," he replied, attempting to tuck his legs up. "And this is the same bike."

Even bunched up in a way that had to be uncomfortable, he was laughing. The sun beamed in lines through the leaves, warming her skin. Away from the bustle of the crowds of yoga mums and BMW-owning dads, she immersed herself in the same feeling of freedom that she'd experienced on the beach that morning. Here there were no judgements or expectations. Her brief argument with Chris had shocked her, but she hadn't run away or had an anxiety attack. She'd never argued with anyone like that before, not even Emma.

She expected him to be angry with her still, but there was no sign of it if he was.

As they cycled through the forest roads, she told

herself to forget her feelings and instead enjoy the moments she got to spend with him. Unfortunately, her body hadn't got the message. Something about Chris made her want to dance on her bike. Her belly was non-stop with butterflies, but it wasn't a sickness. It was like she was glowing with light, yet she was gearing up for the last and most challenging year at school. Their near-kiss during adventure golf was like something from another day. Neither of them brought it up again. Maybe it hadn't been like that. Maybe her family were right, and he was spending time with her to get through the boredom.

"Did you enjoy having chocolate chips on your pancake?" he asked as they rode past a couple of kids and their parents. The parents looked like everyone else, but there was something wide-eyed about the children. It's like they were experiencing everything for the first time. Was it weird to be on the cusp of adulthood and still miss how wondrous everything was? The little children waved at them while giggling, and they waved back as they continued down the road.

"I did. I'm gutted that I didn't get to see the happy face you tried to make on the little squares before I ruined it." Birds tweeted and cooed to each other, but the noise was brief as they continued their travels through the holiday park. A song carried from one of the lodges as Lucie waited for Chris to respond. Did his silence mean he agreed she ruined it?

"You didn't ruin it. You were annoyed, and thankfully the only casualty was a smiley-faced pancake," Chris joked. "Can I let you into a secret?"

"Another one? Sure, I want to learn all your secrets," she replied. She glanced at him briefly before they drove over a hump in the road. His green eyes sparkled in the sunlight, but doubt crossed his face. "You can tell me anything."

"My mum used to make me the best pancakes. My dad tried a couple of times after she left, but it wasn't the same. When she made the fluffiest pancakes in the world, she'd add chocolate chips in a smile. Although sometimes I hate her for leaving us, I miss her too. It wasn't my fault, but I feel guilty sometimes," he said too softly. She slowed her bike and appreciated it when he did too.

"Sometimes I wish my mum would leave my dad, and then I wouldn't have to see him anymore, and then I feel guilty for that," she replied. "We shouldn't though. No matter what happened when you were younger, I bet your mum loved you."

"Yeah, I hope so, but she still left me."

They rode slowly next to each other. The wind rushed through the trees, and sometimes a squirrel or something chattered, but there was no time to distinguish what the sounds were. Chris was silent, occasionally zooming off to execute a perfect wheelie before dropping back to cycle next to her. She couldn't work him out. It was as if there were two sides to him, the honest one who shared things and had a weird childlike nature and the trouble side that needed to act out. That was the side everyone else talked about.

She shook her head, trying to shut out the negative voices of her classmates reminding her that boring Lucie had no sides. "When we were younger, my whole family was on holiday at the seaside in Cornwall. While we were there, Dad got a migraine and stayed home. So on that day, Mum took Emma and me to the beach. It was the best day, and we laughed for hours. We played the 2p arcade machines and jumped up and down in the water. We ate these lush ice creams and chips and performed our silent karaoke game aloud while running in and out of the sea. Dad wouldn't have let us do any of those things. Mum smiled a lot that day. I've never seen her that happy, especially not recently. Dad was grumpy and insisted Mum cooked him dinner when we got home. He was annoyed because we came home smiling and laughing. We hid the things we bought because he would have told us off for wasting money. He really knows how to mindfuck us all."

"That can do a lot of damage. Why does your mum stay with him?"

"Love? Every so often, I catch her holding the crappy plastic keyring we won from the 2p machines, and she has this faraway look on her face," Lucie said. "But what I'm trying to say is our memories are a bit sullied by what we've learnt as we've got older, but like the one with your mum, it doesn't mean these memories mean any the less to us. Maybe it means we should hold them tighter. Don't let what you know now ruin how you felt then."

"You're very wise, Lucie. Do you know that, like properly wise, not the fake kind? I used to believe that adults were always wise and right and had our best interests at heart. But that's bullshit. Don't get me wrong. My dad has always taken care of me and gave me a good life. But he makes mistakes and messes up too. What did my mum think when she left? Dad hasn't been able to talk about it, but they argued a lot before she went. I'd sit on the top of the stairs and listen to them argue. I cuddled my teddy bear, Benji, so hard on those nights, although I was eight years old and too old to be cuddling soft toys. Benji's fur was so soft between my fingers as I cried," he said.

"Have you got another happy memory about her? I

want another one," Lucie requested. Chris stopped by the side of the road and perched on his bike, gazing into the trees. His mouth was downturned, and his sighs carried through the breeze of the forest.

"You sure you want to hear more? I don't want to bore you," he said quietly.

"Bore me? You could never bore me," she replied. His smile gave her belly flutters, and she smiled back.

"Do you remember yesterday when I was surprised at the way you'd drawn my eyes? I thought you'd drawn hers because that was a look she sometimes gave me." Lucie nodded. "The first time I spoke in my school nativity, she gave me that look. I was four, and all I said was, 'There's no room here,' but Mum grinned from the front row, and her eyes were like that."

"That's so lovely."

"Yeah, it was. And then after she treated me to ice cream at this fancy ice cream café near my school. It had booths with bouncy seats. She said I could have anything I wanted. I chose a giant chocolate sundae. Sprinkles everywhere and a wafer on top. As I sat with ice cream smothered around my face, Mum and I laughed about silly things. She made up stories about Father Christmas and the magic he used when he delivered presents around the world. Then, she swore me to secrecy about the ice cream."

"How come?"

"I wasn't supposed to eat sugar, especially not lots of it, because I had a history of vomiting after excess amounts of sugar. Dad worried about me, but the ice cream sundae was as big as my head! I'd forgotten about that day until I saw your drawing."

"Did your dad worry a lot?"

"Yeah, he worried about the days when it was just Mum and me. I never asked him why because I was scared of his answer, but I guess it was hard for both of them in their own way," Chris mused. "No matter what happened between them, I hope Mum is okay and happy wherever she is. I nearly tried to find her once, but I didn't want to ruin the happy memories I have of her."

"I get that. You don't have to make any decisions about finding your mum now. There's lots of time to do it," Lucie replied.

"Yeah, you're right," he said. His shoulders eased, and he leaned his head back and smiled. With the sun on his face, he appeared calmer. How long had he worried about searching for his mum? "I've been thinking about my dad as well. He deserves to be happy. I don't know if he's had a girlfriend in the last ten years, but if he has, I haven't met them."

"Can you imagine him trying to sneak them out of the house before you got up?"

"I'd have heard something, as my bedroom is next to the front door. My dad isn't quiet about anything. When he goes to the loo in the night, he trips over three things and swears each time." Chris laughed. "It wouldn't surprise me if he hadn't dated because he was trying to protect me or something. Maybe he's still in love with Mum. Love does silly things to people."

He glanced at her then and swallowed. His bobbing Adam's apple brought a shiver to her shoulders. She wetted her lips, and his gaze dropped to them. It was like the moment in the trees after adventure golf. Did he want to kiss her? But Emma said he was with her because he was bored, and Emma wouldn't have said that unless she meant it.

Lucie faced away from him and quickly wiped her mouth with the back of her hand in case there was chocolate residue on it. As she turned back, she sneaked a look at her hand. No chocolate. She felt sicker than a five-year-old who'd eaten an ice cream sundae the size of his head, and yet she wanted him to kiss her.

Chris cleared his throat, but his words faltered, and he stared into the distance. Maybe he'd changed his mind about kissing her after she wiped her mouth like that. His gorgeous ex-girlfriend wouldn't have done that. "Anyway, it's always been Dad and me, but he should try dating again. I'd like for him to meet someone. He has a lot of love."

"You must have been lonely when you were growing up. I'm lucky to have Emma. I couldn't ask for a better sister." Emma, or as their favourite teacher called her, "the school's firecracker," burst into Lucie's bedroom every morning to perform breakdancing or body-popping while wearing her pyjama dungarees design. Usually, Lucie insisted on knowing where Emma intended to be in case of an anxiety attack, but she hadn't dared wake her that morning. Would she be angry if she found out Lucie was spending time with Chris? Emma always stood by her side, but Lucie's conversation with her parents and Emma's remarks the night before continued to weigh heavily on her mind.

"Yeah, a bit lonely. I've never talked to someone like this before, but you make it so easy," Chris said, his dimples showing.

Lucie flicked her bangs out of her eyes. "Sorry for judging you earlier. Everyone keeps warning me away from you, and they say—"

"It's okay. I'm used to it."

"But—"

"Lucie," he interjected. "Ever since I was a little kid, I've had this reputation. When I was younger, I'd get into trouble for being too loud in class or answering back when I was meant to be listening. And then when I got to secondary school, I challenged the wrong teacher, and he made my life a sodding nightmare. Maybe now I'd keep quiet, but then it just made me worse."

"But surely the teacher didn't start the rumours?"

"Nah, but it added to the reputation, and I kind of embraced it for a while. I liked how it made people want to be my friend. But they weren't always my friend. When I was about fourteen, fifteen, there was one group who'd dare me to do silly things so they could laugh at me and get me into trouble. A lot of the shit now comes from those days. Dad gave me a talking to, and that helped me sort some stuff out, but the rumours continued and got worse. Like I'm not perfect now and I do crazy stuff."

"Like at the party?"

Chris laughed and rolled his eyes. "Yeah, like that. Like I have this crazy energy to do stupid shit, and I don't always think through it, but having fun is okay. I just wish a teacher at school gave me a chance, but instead they all presumed I was trouble, and it was easier to prove them right even when I was trying not to."

"You're not trouble, Chris. You're amazing." Did she really say that? She changed the subject quickly so he couldn't reply to her compliment. "I'm sorry about your dad. Maybe when you go to university, he will go on dates."

"He'll be able to bring them home then too." He

laughed, although his cheeks carried a pinkish tint too. "Nope, I'm not going there."

"Oh god, I don't want to imagine my parents having sex. When I was at primary school, I thought the fact they had two children meant they'd had it two whole times. I can't believe I thought that. I'm glad I've never heard them do it."

"You probably have, but you don't know it." Chris laughed. His eyes sparkled.

Lucie scrunched her face. "Don't be so gross."

Sex was never going to happen for her. She hadn't even kissed a guy. Lucie had tried to talk to Emma about technique and that moment when you knew what to do. Emma said that it was easy once you were doing it. But if Lucie couldn't kiss, then she couldn't have sex. The thought of being naked in front of someone she fancied made her want to vomit. She hated seeing herself without clothes in the mirror. How could she let anyone else look at her that way?

"Okay, okay. But like, sex is normal." Chris's brow furrowed. "I'm guessing you've never done it?" It wasn't an accusation. He said it casually. People at school made fun of her and how inexperienced she was. How could she be sure Chris was different?

Her heartbeat ramped up, and nausea replaced the butterflies in her stomach. She avoided eye contact, choosing to kick at her bike pedals repeatedly instead. Should she tell him that she'd never kissed anyone? He'd probably laugh. She'd bet there weren't any other seventeen-year-olds that hadn't had their first proper kiss.

Eighteen tomorrow.

It was mortifying.

"Nah, I've never had a boyfriend. Well, not since primary school," she said. She should cycle away and not look back, but even bunched up on his old bike, Chris would catch her.

"Oh, like never, never?" he shouted before quickly trying to cover it up. "I mean, sure. Lots of people don't like to commit and go on dates instead."

If only. No one wanted to date her, and she was probably the only virgin he'd met. How many times would she need to kick her pedal to break her ankle? Then he'd have to take her to the holiday village medic, and he'd forget about her virginity. How many girls had he slept with? Was he joking about the bj rumour yesterday, or had he done that?

His next words surprised her. "Too many people reckon sex is something to tick off a list. But it's not. It's something to enjoy."

Her cheeks were hot again, and she yanked at her ponytail. Would Chris laugh at her if she confessed that she hadn't kissed anyone? Sweat beaded her chest, and her body burnt as if a virus was rampaging inside her. The need to say the words returned, but this was more than asking for chocolate chips. She couldn't tell him she'd never kissed anyone. Maybe she should say it and then ask him out. Then she'd get all the embarrassing stuff out in one go and then could hide forever. But he didn't fancy her anyway, and it wasn't like he'd asked for her number.

"Really? So it's good then? Some girls at school said the first time is awful, but like others have said, it's everything," Lucie's words were running away from her.

"My first time was awkward as hell. My ex was my first, and we had no idea what we were doing. But up until a couple of months ago, it was everything. God, I miss it," he replied, stroking a hand down the back of his neck. Was he saying he'd only slept with his ex?

All the nerve endings in her body tingled at the way he talked. "Yeah?" she asked with a gravelly voice, unsure what else to say.

"Yeah. But people change and move on, and you know, there will be others. In the meantime, I've got my hand to help me along." He laughed.

Lucie squeaked. Was he telling her he masturbated? No one ever talked to her about masturbation, not even the girls at school.

"You okay? You've gone really red."

"I'm fine. I swallowed a fly again or something." She took shaky breaths and gripped the handlebars so tightly that her knuckles turned white. With a push on her pedals, she edged away from him without warning.

Lucie slowly sped up. Her secret burnt her tongue and made her arms quake. Vomit rose in her throat, and tears brimmed her eyes as she imagined him laughing at her as he told his friends about the freak he met on holiday that wasn't just a virgin but had never kissed a guy either. Why was it so difficult to speak this truth to him? He'd told her loads of personal stuff. But every time she considered sharing her lack of experience, she remembered the things her family said. The need to share her truth scraped itself into her skin anyway.

Stop being the boring person everyone believes you to be.

Suddenly she shouted behind her, "I've never had a proper kiss before."

CHAPTER EIGHTEEN

Had Lucie really just told the guy she fancied that she'd never had a first kiss? Surely he'd never speak to her again now? He'd had sex, and she hadn't even kissed someone.

With one glance at his face, she knew he'd caught her words on the breeze. He made an "O" shape with his mouth before nodding and cycling to catch her up.

Admitting the truth made her belly fizz with excitement. Relief rushed through her veins, bringing adrenaline and other mystery things with it. The butterflies were alive again, and she briefly allowed herself to hope that her first kiss would be with Chris. Maybe it was the opportunity to dream or that she'd spoken her mind rather than keeping it locked up, but she suddenly felt reckless. She swallowed hard and let go of her handlebars and rode with her legs.

"Check you out! Daredevil Lucie over there!" Chris laughed deep and loud and removed his hands too. He held them out wide and closed his eyes. His chest expanded as he filled his lungs. Everything about him was gorgeous. Giggles bubbled at her throat.

"You're going to hurt yourself," she said between nervous smiles. She wasn't brave enough to close her eyes like he had. She didn't want to anyway, and with his eyes closed, she admired the way the sun made his skin glow and emphasised the dimples in his cheeks.

He laughed, and she realised he had one eye open. "Nah, I'll be okay. Have you ever had the sun on your face and the scent of pine trees in your lungs as you cycle next to someone cute?"

Oh my god, he called me cute.

Her face flushed. But her inner voice kicked in before she could enjoy it. Cute was what you called your girlfriend's little sister, not someone you wanted to kiss.

"Besides, I'm spreading my wings and changing the world. You should do it too," Chris shouted to the skies.

Something in the excitement bouncing through his words made her want to feel what he was experiencing. Lucie pulled the elastic hair tie from her ponytail and let the breeze whip her hair in the air. Then she eased one eye closed, squinting with the other, and held out her arms. Her hair brushed her cheeks as it flapped around her face. She smiled at the idea that now she couldn't nervously grab her ponytail.

"Your hair is so long," he replied, one eye open, as if marvelling at her mousey brown locks.

She shrugged but refused to be cynical about her hair aloud. It was hard enough riding the bike with one eye open without having to ponder three positives too.

They grabbed their handlebars, and both peddled faster as if racing each other. Trees became blurs, and the only sound was the rush of the wind roaring in her ears. Their bikes grumbled against the roads, straining against the bumps and dips. Lucie was free from the demands of her teachers and parents, and for once, the adrenaline quietened her unconfident inner voice. Nothing mattered, and she powered through the quiet roads of the holiday village. Chris was ahead but occasionally looked back, maybe checking she was with him.

Suddenly up in front, Chris slammed on his brakes. He waved his hands high in the air to get her attention while shouting, "Lucie, stop."

Lucie twisted her bike to the side and squeezed the brakes with a squeal. Gravel kicked up around her tyres. Together she and Chris took in the view as he pursed his lips and gave a long and loud whistle.

"Wow," she whispered. The sight before them was beautiful, but her legs trembled too.

They'd paused at the top of a steep hill. The road continued down to a dip at the bottom. Trees lined the tarmac, and she swore the wind was whistling, "Go back." She wobbled on her bike, unable to take in the prospect of the extreme decline. She'd gain momentum as she fell, and she'd roll until landing at the bottom, her body a mass of broken bones. There were signs to the side telling her it wasn't suitable for bikes. If there were people at the bottom, would they have looked like dots? She wasn't sitting at the top of a hill but the precipice of something significant.

"Do you dare?" Chris asked, staring at her. His green eyes sparkled, and she held her breath as she took him in. A shiver ran up her back, but she wasn't sure if it was from his stare or the hill. "There's no pressure. I'm sure we can ride down there safely, but I'm not going to make you do it. There's a lot more of this forest for us to discover."

"I'm scared," she admitted. Chris held out his hand, and she gripped it tightly. The shivers were all over her skin now. Sickness pitted in her stomach, and her legs shook, making her pedals rattle. She took a deep breath, and as the air left her nose, a tiny smile formed on her lips. "But how can I be the exception if I don't do it?"

He puffed out a chuckle and held her hand tighter. "That was the last thing I thought you'd say. You're amazing. Do you get that? I'm so glad we met, even if it meant your dad shouted at me."

"Me too." She laughed. "Let's hope I make it to eighteen tomorrow, or my dad will be shouting a lot louder at you. He'll write insults on your plaster casts because I won't be able to complete my A-Levels and go to university like he wants me to."

Lucie took another deep breath. Then, between pursed lips, she let all the air out of her lungs. "Come on, Chris. Let's go together."

She released his hand and ran her hands through her hair, temporarily tying it back into its ponytail. Imagine her dying because her hair was covering her eyes. She caught Chris staring at her out of the corner of her eye. His gaze was unreadable, but it made her blush anyway. She was about to plunge to her death with a blushing face.

"Right, let's do this," Lucie whispered. She clipped the waist strap of her rucksack together. Lucie never used it, even when her mum insisted she took a break from studying and joined her on walks in the local countryside. Then she gripped the handlebars tightly and positioned her shimmering blue bike at the top of the hill. Chris did the same, this time fixing his gaze below.

It was no longer the slope of a hill. Instead, it was as if they were at the crest of the steepest mountain with all their fears preparing them for failure.

"We go on three," he said with a shaky voice. His nervousness gave Lucie a smidge of confidence. It was an example of what he'd said before. He wasn't always confident but good at faking it. He was convincing. Although scared, she wasn't on the brink of an anxiety attack. Her pulse was quick but not out of control, and her thoughts were clear. Maybe it was a blip. She'd take time to work out what was going on later.

"Okay," she said breathlessly. "On three."

"One," they said in unison. Be the exception. "Two."

Reach for the stars. You can do this. Be the exception, Lucie.

"Three," they shouted.

She let go of the brakes and began to fly.

CHAPTER NINETEEN

Lucie's ponytail flapped in the breeze.

She reprimanded herself for not wearing a helmet. Would that be her last thought before she died? The road wasn't entirely smooth, and she flew into the air a couple of times before banging back down. Her hands hurt from gripping the handlebars, and her forearms shook when she hit the rough road. The bike rattled, and her eyes watered against the wind. Air rushed in her mouth as she took deep breaths, and she swore something lodged in the back of her throat. She coughed to dislodge it from her mouth and spat to the side, remembering to pick the side that Chris wasn't on. Her heart sped up and was teetering on frantic. This hill was not the place for an anxiety attack.

After a couple of deep breaths, she let go and soared above everything clouding her joy. She glanced at Chris, and he smiled back at her. Her bike wobbled, and she focused on the road. Her fear of falling held tightly to her fear of going back to everyday life. If she'd turned around at the top of the hill and headed a different way, she would have been sitting at her school desk next week hating herself.

Instead, you were brave, and you did it. Pride and wonder overtook her fear.

She imagined Emma at the bottom of the hill, cheering

her on. She couldn't wait to tell Emma all about it when she got back to the lodge. But would she leave out the bit about doing it with Chris? No, she wouldn't. He'd helped her, and they didn't know him like she did. Wasn't that what the naïve girls at school said about their boyfriends before getting hurt?

None of that mattered because he might not want to meet tomorrow. Was this their last day together? Should she force her number on him? What if he handed it back and laughed at her? Thoughts streamed through her mind as she neared the bottom of the hill.

Suddenly she focused on a shape that looked like a tree. Lucie gasped. But it wasn't a tree. It was a real person, and they were waving their arms up and down. They were next to a sign that said "No Entry." Lucie and Chris hadn't seen that from the top of the hill. Had a dip in the road hidden it?

Chris looked back with wide eyes and a grimace. They were careening closer to the man and the "No Entry" sign. His shouts were like whispers. They barely carried over the wind rushing through her ears. Chris mouthed something.

She squinted back and forth at the road.

"Can't stop, don't stop."

"Okay," she mouthed back before clenching her teeth. A spark of happiness surprised her.

As they neared the bottom of the hill, Lucie's bike wobbled out of control. Chris soared past the park ranger, missing him by an inch. The ranger's hat flew into the air as Lucie zoomed past.

"Stop," he hollered. Lucie searched him out, but he wasn't scrabbling for his hat in the dirt; instead, he was chasing them.

"Chris, don't slow down," she called out. "He's trying

to catch us."

Chris must have reduced his speed a little because she suddenly found she was level with him.

He smiled at her before glancing over his shoulder. "Oh my God, he's not stopping. Come on, Lucie."

"You won't get far," the man shouted. He was showing no signs of slowing down. "I'll find you."

Lucie pumped her tired legs a little faster, and Chris did the same.

"He's like Liam Neeson from that movie *Taken*," Lucie shouted at Chris.

Chris's chuckles carried loudly through the woods. "Don't make me laugh, or he'll get us. You're incredible, Lucie. Funny and fearless."

She didn't have time to blush. There was a livid park ranger to shake off. Imagine the trouble she'd get in if he did find her or if he found her dad! She laughed loudly at the idea. *I am trouble too, and I don't care.*

*****

"Oh my God." Chris laughed with her as they ran. "I can't believe we got away from that park ranger guy."

He held her hand as they threaded through the village square, dodging groups of strangers enjoying the late Saturday afternoon sunshine. Her chest hurt from the laughter, but she shrieked with joy as she remembered their adventure.

They ducked past a dad blowing massive bubbles for his toddler, who danced gaily in circles and clapped her hands. "And he chased us for what? Like a quarter of a mile?"

"At least he wasn't Liam Neeson. Imagine what the ranger's skills are."

"He might have cut us in half with a chainsaw," Lucie shouted before they threw themselves into two chairs outside the coffee shop. She laughed between big gasps of air as she attempted to get her breath under control. The clucking of an unimpressed older lady caught her attention. Were people so bothersome that happy teenagers put them off their early evening coffees? She never wanted to be like that.

Lucie refused to let the suppressive nature of the adults in the holiday village get to her as she reminisced about her adventure. The ride down the hill was a mixture of terrifying and enthralling. She'd never felt anything like it. She'd turned her head in the direction of the ranger after they'd sped past him. The hill was behind him and not that high after all. It was her fears making it appear larger than it was.

But if she could do that, then maybe she'd have the confidence to do other things.

A waitress appeared at their table, and they gave their orders.

"I'm so proud of you," Chris said when they'd finally got their breath back. "When you were going down that hill, you were like a superhero."

"It wasn't that impressive," she interjected. Chris raised his eyebrows as if to reprimand her. "Okay, okay. I'm freaking Elastigirl!"

"From *The Incredibles*?" He laughed so hard that his chair wobbled, and he grabbed the table to stop him toppling out of it. "That makes me Mr. Incredible."

That started him laughing again before he began humming the theme tune from the movie. The waitress dropped off their coffees but disappeared quickly. It was a busy time at the holiday village. Everyone from the oldest grandmas to the littlest kids was out having fun.

Chris winked at her and flexed his muscles, setting off her giggles again. She was light-headed from all the happiness propelling through her. Where had those muscles come from? Although he fascinated her, she'd not considered his body too much before. Did he have rock-hard pecs like the guys in boy bands did, or was it a little toned? She chewed her lower lip while imagining it. She covered her mouth with a cough as he grinned back at her. He couldn't know what she was thinking!

"Will you draw as we chat? I love watching you draw," he said gently.

She reached into her blue rucksack and located her drawing pad and pencil. She flicked through the pages, trying to find a blank one, but Chris stopped her on the page with the drawing she'd started of him. "Please, that one," he asked. "I want to keep it when you've finished it."

She ripped it from the spine before dropping the pad back in her bag. Then, with a shy smile, she added shading, aware of his gaze fixed on her. She let the pencil flow across the page. Occasionally she'd take sly looks in his direction to make sure she was incorporating the correct details of his features and because it allowed her to study him.

"I'm going to miss this on Monday when we've gone from here. I met you a day ago, and I can't imagine going to university and not seeing you again." Chris's honesty made her blush. Was he playing games with her? Guys didn't usually display their vulnerability so readily. And yet he'd seen some of hers. Why did her inner voice keep reminding her what her family had said?

"Are you nervous about going?" she asked, avoiding what he'd said and attempting to hide her awkwardness by giving her coffee little blows to cool it down before returning to the drawing. Yet, even with her misgivings, there was a heat to her cheeks.

He tried to hide his face with his cup but she still saw how he twisted his lips. "Yeah. I'm worried about my dad and how he'll be," he admitted.

"And how he'll fit in the time to have all the girlfriends," she quipped.

He laughed, but it was a hollow sound. "Yeah, that. But also, what if I get there and no one wants to be my friend? What if I don't get on with my flatmates or I'm rubbish at my course?"

His vulnerability touched her. He appeared to be the most confident guy in the world, but there were depths there. His head dropped, and he studied the steam coming off his coffee. "Do you know anyone else going to your university?" she asked.

"Not really. I was originally going to go to the same one as my girlfriend—ex-girlfriend—but then she decided uni wasn't for her. So I guess I'm going alone now."

"Oh." Lucie fiddled with her pen, spinning it in circles on the edge of her thumb. "Is that why you broke up?"

"Yeah, but there was other stuff too. We'd grown apart over the last year. Different priorities," Chris said before sipping his coffee.

"Do you still fancy her?" Lucie mentally kicked herself. This sort of questioning was going to get her hurt.

Chris shrugged and looked away. Lucie rolled her eyes when she saw him staring at the group of teenagers that were always close by in the public areas. They played with the hats outside the gift shop, hollering and laughing about something.

Emma had suggested his ex-girlfriend was hot. Anyone dating Chris would be stunning, and lucky too, and Lucie was neither of those things.

"No, I haven't for ages," he finally answered. "And I think I fancy someone else."

He was staring at her. The heat in her cheeks returned, and this time the butterflies in her belly joined it. If Emma hadn't been so against him, Lucie would talk to her and get some advice. Her mum wouldn't help, as she was on her dad's side about Chris. Lucie's lips were sore from all the time she spent chewing them, but she couldn't keep her mouth still.

She squinted against the sun as it appeared from behind the clouds before popping her sunglasses back on. "I get what you mean about uni, by the way. It's okay to be scared, though. I don't want to go back to school and be around people who ignore me or laugh at me. It would be fun if you were with me at school." Lucie moved across to a corner of the page and made swirls and patterns.

"It would be hilarious. I bet we'd get in trouble a lot."

"Especially as it's an all-girls school," she joked, but the sun beat down on her skin. What sort of trouble was he imagining? Sweat beaded her upper lip, and she licked it off. The salt droplets were on her tongue. Did he taste like salt too, or was his tongue sweeter?

"But we'll keep in touch when we leave here, right? We can talk on the phone and text," he added. She smiled but remained fixed on the drawing as she imagined staying friends with him. "You have to give me your phone number. I can't believe I haven't asked you for it before now."

A zip of joy jumped inside her.

"If you get your phone out now, then you can call me, and I'll have it," he replied, eagerly reaching in his pocket.

"I haven't got my phone on me," she confessed. "I got a new phone last weekend, and I haven't learnt the number yet." She nibbled at the inside of her mouth. Did he think she was lying? "It's back at the lodge. My dad doesn't let us have our phones when we go away on our annual September weekend. He has this thing about the weekends being family time. I bet it's to stop us ignoring him or texting about him in front of his face. That is one of Emma's specialities. It's ironic because he's on his phone all the time during weekends at home. He says it's work, but he's probably playing games or something. I should be able to get my number tonight."

"My dad barely uses his phone, but technology isn't his thing. He'd rather be watching football or baking. Not what you'd expect, right?" Chris suddenly added, "Does that mean we can meet up tomorrow? I have a birthday surprise for you."

Lucie's eyes widened as she stared back at him. "Seriously? That would be great. We'll be having family birthday pancakes in the morning, but I should be free from eleven. Shall I meet you on the beach like this morning?"

He nodded keenly, his dimples showing. "Yes, please."

She looked down again, hoping to hide her smiles. Chris wanted to meet again, and he wanted her number.

"Actually." He moved his chair next to hers and sat down. His leg was warm as it brushed repeatedly against hers. He snatched her pencil out of her hand and wrote his number on her paper. "So you have it for when you get your phone back."

"But I thought you wanted this drawing?"

"Oh yeah, well, give me it tomorrow and write the number down again somewhere safe before that."

"Good idea," she whispered as she turned to him. His lips were close to hers, and his eyes were bright and sparkling against the sun. A wisp of her hair danced between them, and he clumsily reached for it and tucked it behind her ears. She gasped as his thumb touched her skin. Her heart thumped against her chest, and a warmth filled her limbs.

"So you can draw without your hair getting in the way," he replied, but his voice had an extra gruffness that hadn't been there before. He no longer smelt of Lynx Africa, but of sweat and suntan lotion. The bustle of thoughts made it hard to focus on any one thing, and so she returned to her drawing to help bring calm.

The swirls she'd been drawing had transformed into a star. When did that happen? She added some feathering to make it a shooting star. "You'll be brilliant at university. Everyone will love you because you're caring and funny. When you get there, you will find a home and the place you belong too. If I can be the exception, then so can you. And if you get scared or unsure or lonely, then you can remember—"

"To spread my wings, reach for the stars, and change the world?" he asked with a laugh. "Like what we said on the beach earlier."

She laughed back. "Yeah, maybe. Or remember you're not alone."

He was still close, but now his arm rested on the back of her chair like they were together. He was staring at her again too. She placed the pencil on the table and lifted her sunglasses so she could meet his gaze. Excitement skittered through her body. A day ago, her fears of the future and how she lived a life she hated consumed her. Most mornings she woke on the brink of tears and worried if today would bring an anxiety attack or passive-aggressive argument with her dad. And now there was Chris. Would she wake up every day thinking of him? Maybe she would wake every morning with a text from him. She smiled despite herself. Should she try and kiss him now, in front of everyone? No, that was a stupid idea. Her first kiss should be in private in case she made a mistake.

He said quickly, "Do you know what you should do?"

Her forehead was tight from furrowing her brow with an unspoken question. Was this the moment? Maybe Chris was going to ask her to go somewhere to kiss. "What?"

"You should confront your dad tonight. You should tell him you're not going to study law, but that you're going to art school instead."

Her chest tightened, and she squeezed her eyes shut. Her legs began to tremble, and her mouth was drying up. She opened her eyes, quickly embarrassed by her reaction, and took a quick sip of her coffee to calm her nerves, but it didn't help. "I can't," she spluttered.

"But you're an amazing artist. Most people will never be as good at anything as you are. You have such a gift. It would be a shame to waste it. Look at what you've done with that star, and that was while you were chatting. You didn't plan it," he carried on.

Her throat was closing now. Where was Emma? She'd be able to calm her. Lucie fought to find words to make Chris stop talking and calm herself down. "It's a hobby. I have to go into law. I have to make my family happy." She pulled her hand out of his. It wasn't working. Her brain was fuzzy, and her pulse sped up. She screwed up the drawing of Chris. She was on the brink of an anxiety attack. Why did her dad have to take her phone away like she was a naughty child? These were the sorts of emergencies she needed it for. What did Emma tell her to do when she was on the edge of an attack? Thought after thought rushed through her, not stopping long enough for her to process each before the next ones bombarded her.

"Why did you do that with the picture? I wanted that, Lucie." Was he upset or disappointed?

Her eyes brimmed with tears, and it was like a hand was reaching for her throat to strangle her. But there wasn't any hand. It was too late to control it. The anxiety attack was coming, and she had to get away. Chris couldn't see it; everyone would laugh at her. The shaking was intensifying, and there were too many things to hide from him. The escalation was rapid.

Shit, please don't let me be sick, not here.

"I have to go," she cried, throwing down the money from her pocket to cover the cost of the coffees. She grabbed her bag and snatched the balled-up paper. How could she tell Chris to reach for the stars when she couldn't talk about her future? She needed Emma. The paper seemed to burn her hand as she scrunched it in her fist. She was a fraud and not an exception. She was a fuck-up, and Chris would hate her if he didn't already.

I hate me.

"Lucie," he shouted, but she was running to the crowds now, desperate to hide the attack from him. "Lucie, don't go."

She threw the paper into the nearest bin, ashamed of

who she was. Today she'd had hope, but now she had nothing.

He shouted something else, but she was too far away. She couldn't see him again.

He knows I'm a freak.

She hated that word, but she'd had the term thrown at her many times. Tears ran down her face as she searched for a space to hide and be alone as the attack consumed her.

CHAPTER TWENTY

PRESENT DAY

"That weekend with you was one of the best of my life," Chris exclaimed, staring at the piece of paper on the table.

The shooting star brought back memories of her anxiety attack under the trees of the forest. As she clawed at her closing throat, she blamed herself for everything. It was as if she'd lost all she'd gained about who she was. Each burst of spirit ebbed away to nothing until, by luck, Emma had walked past and Lucie flagged her down. Emma talked her through the attack, although exhaustion remained for the rest of the evening.

But she'd not thought about what Chris was doing in those first minutes. "I still can't believe you retrieved my drawing," she said.

It was his turn to shrug.

"That weekend changed the course of both of our lives. Didn't it?" Lucie added.

Chris smiled before staring into the distance.

"Yeah, it did," he replied eventually, with a sad sigh. Chris held the paper gently between his hands as he spoke. "That Saturday morning, when we'd stood on the beach, you shared a quote with me. It spoke to my soul. It was simple, the sort of thing that litters Instagram now, yet it opened my mind to possibilities. I've remembered it ever since. 'Spread your wings, reach for the stars, and you will change the world.' I thought about that for a long time. It was like a marble that I would roll around in my brain, trying to see it from different angles as I mulled it over. How could I change the world if I wasn't developing my skills or believing that I had any? I spoke to others about what they thought I should do, and in the meantime, I put my everything into my studies. I was the best student."

"You didn't spend university drunk and joining pointless societies? I'm shocked," she said, trying to bring a smile to his face.

"Well, maybe a little of that too. I was vice president of the extreme frisbee society at one point. I can't even throw a frisbee!" His deep laugh filled her body, and her heart swelled unexpectedly. "Apart from that, I worked really hard, but I was lost in terms of my future. Then one day, when looking at the stars and remembering you and what we went through that weekend, I realised how I could make a difference. You told me that I helped you reach your goals and believe in yourself, from bowling to facing your fears. I had this skill, and I wanted to use it. I became a teacher. Each day, I try and help others to reach for the stars like you helped me to."

"And like you helped me to," she replied without pause. Heat filled her heart at the idea that they had been changing each other's lives from a distance.

He smiled wistfully.

Am I returning his smile, or is he returning mine?

"I did some volunteering after I met you. You inspired me to try," Chris said with a big grin. "I wanted to tell you all about it, but after what happened, I presumed you didn't want to hear from me."

A song by The Weeknd and Ariana Grande came on the jukebox, and she struggled to hide her smile. It had played one night at a bar in Phuket when she was traveling with Emma. Although Lucie had only travelled to Europe during the year before university once Emma finished school and Lucie finished university, they saw the world together. They'd experienced the treasures in Cairo's markets and surfed off the stretch of the Durban coastline.

Her favourite moment was on their last night in Boston, watching *Midsummer Night's Dream* in the park with new friends from around the globe. Lucie hugged Emma tight and sent a thank you to the sky for giving her the opportunities she'd never thought possible before that weekend she'd met Chris. The stars twinkled back at her, and as impossible as it was under the lights of the bright city, she swore she saw a shooting star. Emma joked she'd drank too much beer at the Red Sox game earlier that day, but that moment wouldn't have happened without Chris. Instead, she'd have drowned under a Birmingham law degree.

"Riding down that hill was such a high, especially when that guy chased us." Chris laughed, waggling his fist as the ranger had. "'I'll find you!' Oh my God, my dad fell off a chair in a fit of chuckles when I told him that a couple of weeks later. He was dropping me off at university, and I was worried he was going to cry."

"Your dad laughed?" Lucie asked, trying to envisage the Daniel Craig lookalike belly laughing. "Mine raged."

"Our dads were very different," Chris replied. The conversation lulled into a comfortable silence as they considered the differences between the two men. It wasn't just how they treated their children but in their whole perspective of the world. Thankfully, through Chris, a little of his dad's attitude had rubbed off on her. Lucie took a long sip of her drink and remembered confronting her dad about the art degree.

"That reminds me, I haven't told you where I'm going today," Chris exclaimed, wrenching her from her memories.

Lucie ran her thumb over her tattoo and masked her fears that he was on his way to a significant date. She had no right to hope, especially as she was here to dump Bradley, but she manifested anyway, because the hope that she might have a chance with him brought tingles to her neck and set her heartbeat off on a frantic pace. She hadn't felt like this since… She riffled through her ex-boyfriends, crushes, and significant dates. Each of them had their negatives and their positives, some more than others, but there wasn't anyone that sprung to mind. She hadn't had butterflies flapping in her belly or the desperate urge to smile even though no one had told a joke. The last time she'd truly felt those things was during the weekend she spent with Chris. Maybe it was because he was her first love. But what if it wasn't?

She held her breath, anticipating bad news.

"I've got to get a train to Manchester in thirty minutes because—" He paused dramatically, and she counted to ten to stop herself from reaching over the table and shouting at him to get on with it. "You'll never guess this. It's ludicrous based on eight years ago. But I'm off to Manchester because my dad is getting married!"

She exclaimed a laugh, although it was more from relief than the news of a wedding. She gulped a deep breath and took her time in formulating a more

147

appropriate response. "Your permanently single dad is getting married? That's the best news ever. Do you like her? How did they meet? You have to tell me everything."

He leaned closer. Lucie was both relieved and disappointed he didn't smell like Lynx anymore. It wouldn't be appropriate for a man his age, but she missed the response that came with the smell. Even now, when she caught a whiff, which was usually when she was in the local shopping centre on a Saturday afternoon, her belly would flutter and her heart beat a little faster. She always turned to check if it was Chris, which, of course, it never was. It was difficult to hide her disappointment from being confronted by a pimply-faced teenage boy with tight jeans and a bizarre hair quiff. Chris never looked like that, thank God.

Chris's excitement was palpable, and she recognised the teenager she met in the forest who was vulnerable, caring, and funny. The hope that she might have a chance with him brought tingles to her skin. Seeing this version of him reminded her of the happiness that lived in her long after that weekend. Lucie gulped a deep breath.

"He's marrying the mum of one of my students. It's sweet and yet kind of awkward how they met. A couple of years ago at the school where I teach, I directed a musical comedy version of *Romeo and Juliet*—don't ask. It wasn't my idea."

Lucie giggled. Talking animatedly with extra winks and dramatic hands was the Chris she remembered.

"Anyway, Dad volunteered to come and stay for a month and take charge of construction on the set. Before he arrived, the students were using cardboard scenery, but Romeo thought it would be funny to start a water fight on stage, and that was the end of that. Sarah, the mum of the student playing Juliet, also offered to help. At first, Dad and Sarah argued a lot."

"That doesn't sound like your dad. I thought he was chilled out," Lucie replied.

"That's true. To be fair, my dad sat and worked away, and she argued with him. He was oblivious to her worries and focused on his work. It's continued to be one of his adorable yet frustrating traits. One evening Dad hammered his thumb, and although he was very blasé about it, Sarah took him to the hospital. The next day he brought her in some cupcakes he'd made, and love blossomed from there."

"Wow, so you had a real-life Romeo and Juliet, but without the depressing ending. That is perfect." Lucie imagined the scenario and sighed happily.

"It was the one positive thing to come out of that whole show." Chris's laugh was infectious. "There was another injury. One student had their first ride in an ambulance on opening night when the fight scene got out of hand. Mercutio was getting off with Tybalt's girlfriend in the wings while Tybalt was on stage. It all kicked off, and instead of a humorous Charleston fight scene, we had blood everywhere from a broken nose while several parents wailed about their 'poor little' seventeen-year-old lads, the same lads who were lamping each other with more vigour than I'd seen from them during any rehearsal. The headteacher hasn't asked me to direct any more shows since."

"I can't imagine why," Lucie joked.

He shrugged, but his eyes twinkled, and his smile showed his dimples. "Anyway, Sarah is the best thing to happen to Dad. She has brought out of him this happiness

I've never seen before. He was always lovely, but now he doesn't care if he makes a fool of himself because if it makes her laugh, then it's worth it. He's great with Annie, Sarah's daughter. She's now at university. Dad and Sarah moved to Manchester a year ago, and now they're getting married there too."

"That's amazing. I'm so happy he found love after everything your parents went through," Lucie said with a wistful smile.

"All the demons that he had after Mum left have gone. There was a lot of fear and mistrust bundled up in his relationship with Mum. It wasn't all Mum's fault. They were too young, and Mum didn't have the right support."

"How do you know? Did he finally talk about her?"

"I searched for Mum," he replied quietly. Lucie held her tongue and gave him space to talk. "One weekend, I decided to find out everything. I received cards every birthday from my grandma, so I started with her. I met with Gran, a woman I hadn't seen since Mum left, and she told me some of it. Mum and Dad met on the night of Mum's eighteenth birthday. Mum was at college, and Dad was a bouncer at the local club. Mum's dad recently died, and instead of working through her grief like everyone was trying to make her do, she started a relationship with a guy who she decided would make everything better."

"Your dad?"

"Yeah," Chris replied, fiddling with the flyer for a local club that someone had discarded on the table. "The problem is that Mum had mental health problems that escalated after her dad died. But she refused help for them too. She believed my dad could be her hero, but that wasn't what she needed. Within six months, she was pregnant with me—again, not what she needed, but you can't blame either of them. She was young and not the first to believe a baby would solve her problems. She developed depression and then other stuff after that, including panic attacks. Mum didn't have any help and avoided her family. She sunk deeper into depression. She had good days, those I remember fondly, but other days she couldn't get out of bed."

"Like that time you busted your nose?" Lucie cut in.

"You remembered that?"

"Of course," she replied. She remembered everything Chris said that weekend.

"Yeah, that was one of her bad days. Dad didn't know what to do, and he had no experience of mental health issues. People didn't talk about it as much as they do now. They argued a lot, more than I knew. They'd no clue how to bring up a child, let alone deal with anything they were going through. Then, one day, Mum decided that she needed help and that without it, she was making things worse. She was so scared. She loved me so much and was scared that she would have a dangerous panic attack when driving or something. It wasn't like that, and I was never at risk, but those were her fears. So she left." Chris lifted his head, and Lucie took his hand in her spare one. There were tears in his eyes, but he didn't wipe them away or get embarrassed. "Mum never stopped loving me."

"Of course not. It was lovely that your grandma filled in those gaps for you," Lucie said, squeezing his hands. "I'm so glad you were able to learn about her from your gran. Did she give you photos?"

"I got better than that. I met my mum," he replied. He smiled even as a tear slipped down his face onto his shirt. "She works at a centre in London for people with depression. She trained as a counsellor, and now she helps people because that was how she worked stuff out for herself, and she wanted to give back. Mum carried the guilt of leaving and not returning for years. Occasionally she'd find her way to town and watch Dad pick me up from school or, a couple of years later, see me exit the gates with friends and considered saying hello, but she was scared of how that would impact me."

"I can't believe it. Your poor mum must have gone through so much, and yet she used that to help others. You're definitely her son." Lucie wiped the remaining tears from his eyes with her thumbs before holding one of his hands again.

"Yeah, I am." He grinned. "But thank you for saying it too. Mum and I speak on the phone every couple of weeks, and I've visited her a couple of times during the school holidays. It's made it easier to understand Dad too. He carried his guilt for a long time. He believed he hadn't tried hard enough to fix her or pushed her away too quickly, but now he gets it. She didn't need him fixing her, but she needed professional support. They've met and talked through everything," Chris replied with a sigh of relief and a smile that twisted his lips to the side. It made him appear ten years younger and reminded her of how young they'd been when they met.

Suddenly one of the glass clearers bumped into Lucie and snatched the empty wine glass from the table. It was as if he'd broken the spell between them, and Lucie dropped Chris's hands in surprise.

"Thanks," the guy said as Chris passed his empty bottle over.

"And now your dad is getting married," Lucie said

after the guy disappeared.

"Yes, he is. I'm freaking over the moon for him. And I'm going to be the best man, so whatever happens, I can't miss the train. My school have allowed me the afternoon off. I came straight from a lesson, and like the classy man I am, I changed in the station toilets. Am I presentable enough for a wedding?" he asked, standing up beside her chair. "I struggled a bit with my tie. I've never been very good with them. Maybe it's punishment for wearing them around my head when I was a rebellious teenager."

Lucie giggled at the image. "Can I?" she asked.

He nodded and smiled broadly enough to show his dimples. Lucie stood and wrapped her hands around his tie. The silk caught the rough skin near her cuticles. She'd been nibbling them on the train this morning before she'd listened to one of her mindfulness recordings.

Slowly she smoothed the tie down before reaching up and giving the knot a wiggle so that it was a little tighter. Standing close to Chris, she was able to breathe him in. The smell of Lynx may have gone, but the scent that filled her body nearly made her sigh aloud. It was a heady scent, a mixture of leather and citrus with a hint of spice. It was the scent of men in contemporary romance books. Maybe he was wearing his best fragrance for the wedding.

The sudden urge to find out if she had a hope of being with him overwhelmed her. It was as if a giant wave of nervous heat filled every limb as she contemplated her words. The question burnt her tongue, and flames filled her mouth. She wasn't the shy Lucie from all those years ago, so why was she terrified of uttering the words?

"I was wondering," she said as she fiddled with the collar of his shirt. She stretched her neck, moving her head from side to side. The movement was a tactic to distract her overthinking brain. It was an unusual move, but it offered the opportunity to ask things without her anxiety silencing her. "Are you seeing anyone?"

CHAPTER TWENTY-ONE

That nausea that accompanied a lot of Lucie's significant moments with Chris returned. She was in a "relationship", and yet she'd asked if he was single. What difference would it make? First loves never worked out. Stretching her neck from side to side as a distraction technique only worked for so long. She swallowed nervously and fixed her gaze on his tie, pretending to locate and pick off a piece of lint. She might as well have still been seventeen from the mix of emotions threatening her cool. Chris tucked his finger under her chin and lifted it so that her eyes met his.

He shook his head. "No, I'm free and single." His lips lifted in a smile that brought a rush of joy. It replaced the queasiness that ruled her body. But he hadn't finished talking. She desperately tried to hide the tremble threatening to give away her thoughts.

His finger warmed the little dip beneath her chin. She wanted to lean into it. She bit the inside of her mouth to stop all the urges willing her forward. She was more impulsive these days, but so much had happened in their lives since that weekend. It was impossible to believe they could return to those days flush with first love.

He smiled nervously at her before adding, "I guess, for a long time, I was searching for someone a bit like you."

She wasn't sure what to say. It was how she felt too. There were guys, including Bradley, but it hadn't felt right with them, like it had felt with Chris. But she'd carried on trying to live a "normal" life, dating and trying different experiences while reminding herself regularly that she couldn't stop her life for a guy she knew for one weekend. But those guys hadn't compared to him, and deep down, she'd carried the hope that one day she'd meet Chris again and that he wouldn't hate her for how their weekend ended.

"Are you seeing anyone?" He stuttered through the question.

"It's complicated, but yes, I am dating someone," she replied, wincing when his shoulders fell. She slid back into the booth, unable to meet his eyes. He followed her lead and sat too. Once again, they were opposite each other with a shabby table separating them. "But you hit the nail on the head when you said this is the place people come to dump the people they're dating. Bradley and I aren't serious. I've wanted to break up for a while. I waited until now because of the job interview, and because most of my relationships tail off naturally because they're not what I want." Did she sound like she was trying to justify herself? It was the truth, and she was pretty sure Bradley saw it coming. He wasn't all in and never had been.

"Okay," Chris said quietly. Lucie attempted to decipher the emotions behind his eyes. Most people kept their first love in the past for a reason. They were two random people who liked each other when they were teenagers. People grew up and changed. If that was true, why did the thought of not seeing him again scare her more than her job interview that morning?

Lucie cleared her throat. "And because I was too scared to confront him. I guess I'm not that different from scared eighteen-year-old Lucie after all."

Chris shook his head. "You were strong in many ways that weekend, and everything I've seen so far shows me that you're even stronger now. You'll do it. Your fears are high right now, and I get that."

Lucie blushed and tapped her fingers against the table. She touched a tacky bit and blanched as she searched for something to wipe her sticky fingers on. She needed to change the subject. "By the way, I can't believe what you did for my birthday on the Sunday of our weekend. That present and the way you helped me was more significant than you'll ever believe. It changed everything," she said, now fiddling with the flyer he'd had before. Chris stared at her with a furrowed brow. What was he thinking about? "You made me laugh a lot that day too."

"You deserved a great day, and I'll never forgot that moment on the high ropes," he said with a slight shiver. "How have the anxiety attacks been? I have a student who is going through something similar, and she's been struggling. I told her about you and the things we discussed. She wanted to meet you, but I didn't know where you were."

She smiled at the memory of that Sunday. "I can control them by myself now. I still get them, but I have tactics to calm down that mostly work. I don't need Emma anymore. Can I share one of the tactics with you?"

He nodded keenly.

"It's called a self-soothe bag."

She had no fear in showing him the bag as she had with guys in the past. When one of her boyfriends found it, she'd locked herself in the bathroom, terrified that he'd laugh at her. Why had she stayed with guys when she expected that reaction over her anxiety? She reached into her handbag and pulled out the small canvas bag decorated with pink and black flowers and with a steampunk edge to it. Holding the canvas brought her instant calm.

Lucie tucked her finger into the loop of the drawstring as she spoke. "Some people use a box, but I wanted something compact when I went travelling. One of my art college friends designed this bag for me. The idea is that you put things inside that can be meaningful and helpful. There has to be a range of things so that you can tap into your five senses. Then by touching or tasting, for example, you can ground yourself. It doesn't always work, but it is one of the most effective things I've found."

She briefly looked up and marvelled at the wide-eyed stare of Chris. He appeared fascinated by the bag she placed on the table.

One by one, she retrieved different items from inside.

"These are my headphones for when I need to shut out the world. I have a playlist on my phone called 'For fuck sake stay chill.'" Lucie laughed gently as she reached for another item. "This is a fidget spinner that has been all around the world with me. Some people think they're childish but—"

Chris pulled a fidget spinner out of his jacket pocket with a smile, cutting her words short. "Snap. I use mine when I need a distraction from some of the drama at school. They discovered at university that I'd always had ADHD. This thing helps me to focus. I give it to the kids at school as well when they need to chill."

She smiled back shyly. She'd considered speaking to

her own doctor about being neurodivergent after some of the stuff that had come up recently with professionals around her anxiety groups and discussions she'd had with Emma. Did this explain their unfathomable connection? Maybe it was why being around him put her at ease and yet filled her to the brim with nervous energy.   She hastened on. "I also have this tiny teddy bear. I picked it up at a gift shop in America. It reminded me of a bigger one I would cuddle when I was little, and Mum would read me bedtime stories."

"I love this. Thank you so much for sharing it with me," Chris replied as she grabbed postcards from her travels, a worry doll from Guatemala, and pictures she'd drawn in various places. The bag also included a couple of lollies, a fruity lip balm, and chocolate.

"Emma made this for me," she said, showing him a crystal star. It hung on the end of a necklace. It was an original and bespoke piece, and Lucie often held it and reminded herself of all the supportive things Emma said to her.

There were three more things in the bag. Lucie hesitated before getting them out. "Promise you won't laugh at these last items?"

Chris tilted his head to one side and stared at her. His green eyes were beguiling. "Why would I laugh?"

She shrugged and warily pulled out a stone. She considered lying about the dull piece of rock. It was rubbed smooth by her fingers over the years. "It's from that weekend," she blurted, although she was unsure why.

The last item was a birthday candle. "This was from our last day together," he exclaimed before rubbing his thumb over it. "I wondered what happened to it."

"You made it such a special day," she said, imagining

159

his thumb smoothing over her bottom lip in the same way as he leant into kiss her. But it was just a fantasy. Her stomach twisted in helplessness. Their Sunday together had been a special day until it ended so painfully. Would they ever get around to talking about what had happened?

She moved the bag, needing to keep her hands busy. It rattled against the table.

"There's something else inside your bag," he said quickly. There was no fooling him. "You must have missed an item. What is it?"

Reluctantly Lucie's hand went back in the bag and grasped the last item, a travel-sized deodorant. Chris reached across the table and took it from her. "Lynx Africa. Wow, I haven't used this in ages. Can I?" he asked with his finger on the button. She nodded slowly.

At the *psssss* sound, Lucie was transported back to her last day with Chris in the forest. What if events had unfolded differently? Would they have spent the previous years together, or was it true that everything happened for a reason? Sometimes she believed the saying was right, but then could it be mindless words offered to help people filled with sadness and regret.

"I can't believe I used to smell like this," he said with a broad smile.

"I liked the way you smelt," she whispered, her gaze entirely focused on the table.

"Did you put this in the bag because of me?"

How should she answer that? She couldn't tell him she'd loved him all this time. Instead, she shrugged before hurriedly gathering the items and hiding them back in the bag. "Anyway, I'd love to meet your student and tell her where I got help and show her how to make one of these, although you can find it on the internet too. At university, I joined some forums, and I learnt a lot about anxiety and how to manage it. Since then, I've run meetups for teenagers struggling through it." She was proud of those who'd improved and gained resilience. "There's a lot of support out there. The most important thing you can tell your student is that she's not alone, and although she feels like it's never going to be okay, there's hope. I can put her in touch with some great support groups if you want? Chris, you helped me on my journey of getting help. It sounds cheesy, but it's true."

Chris shrugged with a half-smile.

"Seriously, don't underestimate it."

He grinned, and she marvelled again at his dimples. As a teenager, he'd stolen her heart with his boyish good looks, caring attitude, and goofy persona. But now he was a gorgeous man who still carried that air of amusement and love for others. She pushed away from the sadness. What if their weekend hadn't ended as it had? Would she have watched him turn into a man and had the opportunity to enjoy their life milestones together? Their first university ball, their first sunset in a different continent, moving in together. She'd had some of them with others, but with Chris, they would have meant something. At least she'd seen him again. But was it one chance meeting and then they'd go on with their lives and never see each other again?

"Lucie, you helped me too. You gave me the confidence to go to university. I was intent on dropping out. None of my friends from home planned to go, and I presumed I wasn't good enough to be going either. Total imposter syndrome. I thought I'd arrive and the university chancellor would send me home, or in the middle of a lecture, I'd get found out as a fake and the other students would laugh as security ejected me from the room." He reached for her hands, cradling them between his own. "You helped me through that."

Lucie's words caught in her throat, and she swallowed noisily. "You told me your insecurities, but to me, you were the coolest guy who could handle anything. I didn't doubt that you would be amazing," Lucie replied, enjoying the warmth from his hold. Occasionally the fan of the air conditioning breezed down her back, but sitting here with him, she'd never felt so cosy.

"You saw things in me that I hadn't until that weekend. Meeting you meant I went to university, and I attended every lecture and read all the books recommended and extra ones too. I took the time to learn and immersed myself in the whole experience. I have no idea what my future would have been without you, but it wouldn't have been this. I had to put the effort in, but you made me realise that I could do it," Chris said earnestly. "I wanted to tell you about my experience at university and share the funny and unusual things that I learnt about in psychology but also the interesting people I met too. I thought about you a lot and wondered which of my stories or things I'd learned would make you laugh or gasp and which of the people you would choose to draw. Sometimes a lecturer would do something funny, or I'd eat a pancake and want to tell you about the toppings on offer. I've missed you."

Lucie smiled softly. "I never doubted you. Once you found your passion, I knew you'd give it everything you had. You had this light about you, and I couldn't get enough of being around you. I've missed you too." She wetted her lips. She wanted to kiss him. His eyes dipped to her lips. Was he thinking the same thing?

The pub where people went to dump their lovers wasn't the place for a kiss, and how cruel would it be to Bradley? She needed to get on with it and ditch him, and somehow, this time with Chris reminded her that she didn't need to be scared. She closed her eyes and took a breath. "Let me get us another drink. What do you want?"

"It's okay, I'll get them," he replied, fishing through his pockets.

She took the opportunity to flick her bangs out of her face. Beneath her eyelashes, she looked at him. "Before I lose confidence, I have to tell you that you did loads for me too. I'll never be able to share everything, but one thing in particular springs to mind. About four years ago, Emma and I passed an old church hall in a little town near Auckland in New Zealand. There was music, like something from a vintage radio. I dragged Emma into the hall with me, and we danced for hours at this little social club. There were loads of strangers who had questions about our travels and what brought us to their little town."

"That sounds amazing."

"It was. As I danced with the older men and women, I asked them for their stories, especially how they met their partners. I've been a sucker for a good love story since, well, since my eighteenth birthday." A tingle crossed her neck at his smile. "One woman, Edith, shared much of her life. She told me that it had been nearly a year since her husband died. They were together for sixty years before he died of cancer. She was now at the point that she didn't feel she could talk about him anymore because it was so long since he'd gone, and people were bored of hearing about him."

"That's so sad."

"I know. A tear ran down Edith's cheek as she told me that she missed him every day, from the moment her alarm clock woke her to the last minutes in bed when she'd turn to the side he used to sleep on and whisper goodnight. She talked about him throughout our next three dances. We remained friends. Edith and I still speak on the phone, and every time we do, she has an old story about her husband. Sometimes we laugh, and sometimes we cry, but every time she speaks, it's like her love of him fills every word."

Chris stared at her, his green eyes unmoving. His lips raised at one side in a tentative smile, but he didn't speak. Lucie rubbed her hands to warm them. It was the first chill in her fingers since they'd arrived.

"The day I met Edith, I told her the thing you said on our last day together. I still get goosebumps now. 'Life changes us, but nothing changes us more than falling in love. Our soul keeps the person safe in our hearts, and we carry their imprint for the rest of our lives. Unless they're arseholes, and then they can bugger off.' Edith found the last part particularly funny," Lucie added with a smile.

Chris's mouth opened, but he didn't say anything. His eyebrows dived together, but he didn't ask his question.

"Are you okay?" she asked, resting her hand on his arm. He flinched slightly. His features sunk in front of her. There were no dimples on his cheeks and no joy in his downturned mouth. His eyes had lost their sparkle. Lucie moved to remove her hand, but Chris reached for it and held it in his. Emptiness replaced the fluttering in her belly.

Chris gripped her hand tightly as he spoke with a shaky voice. "I have to know, Lucie. What happened on that Sunday? Did I do something wrong? Why didn't we keep in touch?"

CHAPTER TWENTY-TWO
EIGHT YEARS EARLIER, SUNDAY

Lucie sucked air into her mouth before yawning so wide that her cheeks hurt. It was another sleepless night spent tossing and turning in bed. Thank goodness she wasn't sharing a room with anyone. Emma, who accepted most things Lucie did, would have jumped on her midway through the night at her relentless grumbles of frustration. One thought rumbled around her head, shrouding all others until it was all she considered. Would Chris be waiting for her on Sunday morning?

The question impacted her movements from the moment she got out of bed until she was ready to join her family downstairs. It was Chris she imagined as she attempted to put waves in her hair before she huffed and fisted the strands into a ponytail. It took half an hour of debating between outfits before she selected a pair of mid-thigh jean shorts that Emma lent her that revealed more skin than her routine long ones. Would her mum comment on her legs like before? She reached for the cotton dress that Jess had offered her and held it up against her body as she stared at her reflection in the full-length mirror. She didn't have the same frame as Jess, and there was the problem with her legs too. Did Chris prefer women who wore dresses?

He wasn't going to be there anyway. Why would he come back after she'd run away from him? She looked at the dress again with its thin shoulder straps and above-the-knee length. She gave it one more stroke before returning it to the bed. It was the first time in years she was tempted to wear a dress, but she wanted to be practical in case she headed into the forest on her bike. And she wanted to be herself even if he didn't show up.

A balloon bounced across the floor and nearly tripped her up as she reached the bottom of the stairs. Eighteen years old. She almost forgot. She could do anything and be anything she wanted to be. She'd never considered that before. She didn't have to be what her dad told her to be.

Lucie took a deep breath and let the realisation take hold. A smile touched her lips, and the tips of her fingers tingled. It was her birthday, and today she could draw and do whatever she wanted. The tingles stretched through her hands and up her arms. She'd create something beautiful.

"Those bags under your eyes are massive," her dad muttered from the sofa. He sat wide-legged in the lounge area of the open-plan lodge. Was he trying to display dominance or stop people from sitting with him? It didn't matter because he didn't get to ruin her day. Jess's parents, Steve and Jacky, sat on the other sofa, deep in conversation, until her dad dropped his insult. Did she catch an eye roll from Jacky? "You are getting old now. Thank goodness you don't need to rely on your looks."

He winked at Steve with a smug grin. Another comment aimed at crushing her confidence and making him the big man. But not today. Jacky rushed over and embraced Lucie, eclipsing the words her dad attempted to hurt her with. "Happy birthday, sweetheart," she said before whispering in her ear, "And don't listen to your dad. You're a lovely and talented young woman."

"Brains and beauty, you've got endless amounts of both. With your art skills, you're a force to be reckoned with," Steve bellowed, facing her but talking loud enough for her dad to hear. He offered her a box wrapped in pink foil wrapping paper with a shiny blue bow on top. It crinkled when she clasped it tightly between her hands. She smiled back at the couple. They were kind. Steve probably teased her dad too much, but Lucie understood why. If she could get away with it, she'd probably throw some digs his way as well. "It's from Jacky and me. Something to help with your talent."

"Thank you. That means a—" she whispered, but her dad cut her off.

"Art skills? There's better drawings in primary schools." He laughed loudly, but no one joined in. "Besides, she won't have time to play around with her crayons because she's going to be studying hard for years."

Lucie used to make excuses for him and say that she could have a worse dad. But why was she letting him off? Just because he wasn't hitting her didn't mean he was a good dad. The family set him a low bar, and he barely reached it. It was time she recognised what he was like and treated him as such. He didn't deserve to have two kind and talented daughters. They weren't a testament to anything he did. His genes were a detriment rather than a blessing. His contribution to her life, and Emma's, was to crush their confidence and, in her case, bring anxiety issues. At some point, he'd given away his opportunity to be loved and respected.

Lucie opened her mouth to share this with him. Heat

filled her, and the shaking of her body was visible. She wasn't his victim. A roaring filled her ears, and her tongue was on fire. It didn't matter that it was her birthday morning, because some things needed to be said.

"Happy birthday to you," her mum sang as she danced into the room from the downstairs bedroom. It quickly killed the tension. Every birthday, her mum would do a jig. The jig was haphazard, with no specific moves other than a shake of the bum and a bounce of her arms as she sang the happy birthday song.

The sound of a herd of elephants rumbled through the lodge as Emma and Jess ran down the stairs. They sang and giggled. Lucie's anger disappeared and was replaced by laughter as Steve, Jacky, Emma, and Jess joined in with her mum's jerky moves as they sang and shimmied around her.

There was a grunt from the direction of her dad as he rolled his eyes and stormed off. Was it because he hated the dance or because he wasn't the centre of attention? It didn't matter. Instead, Lucie joined in with the dancing and waved her hands in the air. It was how she wanted to start her eighteenth birthday, and her dad's absence made it nearly perfect. But, of course, there was another person she wanted to sing happy birthday to her, but after yesterday, that dream was impossible.

*****

Lucie's shoulders trembled as she popped the last piece of pancake in her mouth. Little children giggled over their breakfasts. Clown-faced helium balloons loomed from the tables and seemed to follow the waiters as they walked past before returning to bob for the families at their table.

"Those balloons are terrifying," Emma whispered in

her ear. "You okay?"

Lucie grimaced as she nodded back.

But it wasn't the balloons that made her tremor or the screams from babies and their toddler siblings. It wasn't even her dad's persistent huffing and grumbling to remind everyone he was unhappy Lucie chose the noisy pancake house for her birthday breakfast and sour-faced from the fun in the lodge that morning.

Her nervousness was because it was nearly eleven o'clock. Was Chris waiting outside for her, or was she about to find out he was gone from her life forever?

Remembering what had happened when she'd bolted from Chris was a chink in the joy of the meal. Her embarrassment had dogged her throughout the morning. Everything reminded her of him, from the place where she'd hidden after her attack to the bowling alley where he'd helped her. The cookie cutter families who rocked their babies in time with each other while doom scrolling on their phones reminded her that she didn't have Chris's number anymore.

She'd made an idiot of herself. In the light of day, when the threat of an anxiety attack wasn't chasing her heels, her reaction seemed bizarre. It had to be weird to him too. Thank goodness Emma had talked her down before they saw their parents.

"Excuse me."

A familiar-looking grey-haired man stood at their table. His face resembled leather from too many days spent in the sun. His green uniform clung to his body as if he'd already sweated through his clothes. It was the ranger.

"What do you want?" her dad asked. The ranger

stiffened. Her dad had once explained to Lucie and Emma that menial staff had those jobs because they were incompetent and stupid and should be treated as such. She hadn't considered it before. But Lucie's guilt from her treatment of the ranger the day before climbed when she saw how her dad treated him now. Was she as bad as her dad?

"I wanted to have a word with this girl about her reckless bike riding yesterday. Not only did she ignore a No Entry sign, but she nearly ran me over and continued riding without an apology. I could have been seriously hurt."

"Lucie," her mum gasped, making an already uncomfortable situation a million times worse. "Is this true?"

Lucie's cheeks heated as she shrugged her shoulders. "I didn't see the sign when I started riding down the hill, and then I couldn't stop. It doesn't need to be a drama."

"Doesn't need to—"

"But of course, I am sorry," she added, cutting her dad off. "I'm sorry…"

The ranger offered his name. "Vincent."

"Vincent, I genuinely am sorry. I was caught up in the moment of doing something thrilling and then realised I was unable to stop. I should have found you afterwards, but as I say, it was a bit of a moment, which is no excuse, but I'm sorry for any distress I may have caused you. You were only doing your job."

Maybe she'd taken the wind out of his speech because Vincent smiled. "That's okay. That hill is a bit deceptive, and maybe we should add a sign at the top. You and your young man were having a good time. I, too, remember being young and riding down steep hills without a care in the world."

"Your young man?" her dad asked angrily.

Vincent wrung his hands. "I hope I haven't said anything I shouldn't. I'll leave you to your day. Please stay away from steep hills."

Her dad glared at her as Vincent headed out of the pancake house. "Did you recklessly endanger that poor man's life to impress a boy? Don't dare tell me it's the same boy from the bowling alley."

"I wouldn't dare, Dad," Lucie replied with a bit of sass. Emma choked on her juice.

"First, you cut Dad off, and then this," Emma whispered between gasps of air.

"That had better not be an attitude. Your lack of respect is disgusting, Lucie."

"Apologise to your dad for your attitude, Lucie," her mum jumped in. Lucie rolled her eyes.

Why was her mum always on his side when he treated her so appallingly? This weekend had reinforced her belief that her parents didn't have her best interests at heart. It was as if the blinkers had dropped from her eyes and she was witnessing how clueless they were.

"I'm sorry if you felt my attitude was inappropriate, Father," Lucie replied. Emma's mouth dropped.

"You are out of order. I could cancel the rest of your day and send you back to the lodge to study. But I don't believe this is the real you speaking. That boy is to blame, and I forbid you from seeing him again. You will spend today alone, considering your behaviour. When I see you again this evening, I expect a formal apology and a visible change in your behaviour. Are you listening to me?"

But she wasn't. Instead, a figure on the beach caught her eye. Even without the detail of his green eyes and dimples, she knew it was Chris. He'd come for her. She'd go to him no matter what her dad said, but she had to hide it from her family.

"Okay, Dad. I shall do all the things you say. We should pay. It's getting busy," she said, drawing his attention away from the window. He hated groups of "ordinary people," as they often led him to act out and stand out from the crowd so as not to appear as regular and middle class as everyone around him.

They all stood. Her dad headed immediately for the till, as he refused to pay the bill at the table. Emma's brow furrowed as she picked up on Lucie's sudden change.

Anxiety itched at Lucie's skin as she sought to keep her parents from seeing Chris.

"What are you girls doing today?" her mum asked as they walked through the pancake house.

"I'm meeting Jess at the swimming pool in ten minutes. We're going on the flumes twenty times. The wave machine too!" Emma replied. Any other fifteen-year-old would shrug and suggest they were going to be bored. But not Emma. She was proud of her love of flumes and wave machines and all the other things that made ten-year-olds squeal. She didn't care what people thought or what others her age were doing.

"And how about you, Lucie? Are you going with them?" their dad asked. "You have one more day of freedom before school and the hard work begins. You should spend it with your sister rather than get into trouble."

Anger dripped through her veins. He thought that by forcing her to be with Emma, she'd behave? Since when had Emma become the good daughter? Lucie fought the temptation to huff or lay into him. And he'd got that comment about school in. That she had no answer irritated her further. She glanced at the window, but Chris was still on the beach, facing the water. She'd never lied about something significant to her parents before.

"Or you could spend it with your dad, me, and Jess's parents. We've booked Outdoor Bowls, tennis, and then we're going to go into the depths of the forest to spot the different trees. You're too late to book the sports, but watching is exciting too," her mum said enthusiastically. It would have been endearing, but the faux excitement was for her dad's benefit. The activities had him written all over them. "And it's always nice to learn about the trees. You could help us spot the different types."

She needed to spend the day with Chris. An unexpected ache filled her chest.

The handsome waiter from the previous day said hello as they were paying the bill at the till. "No chocolate chips today?"

"No." Lucie blushed. Her face heated as her family stared at her.

"She's too old for chocolate chips," her dad responded. "She's not a child."

The waiter offered a reassuring smile. "You're never too old for chocolate chips," he said as her dad used the card machine.

"That's true. I shall make a smiley face on my pancake with chocolate chips next time," Lucie said loudly, grinning when her dad huffed and headed for the door without leaving a tip. Emma and her mum followed him while thanking the waiter.

It wasn't right that her dad didn't leave a tip when he could afford it. Lucie fished through her purse and popped some money next to the till. "Thank you," she said to the waiter, who smiled back as she rushed to follow her family out the door, trying to stop them before they saw Chris.

She reached them as they left the dimmed lighting of the pancake house. Sunshine glinted off the pathways and briefly blinded her. Would Emma cover her if she pretended she was spending the day swimming with her and Jess? She glanced at the beach again as trembles filled her fingers.

The ache of not seeing Chris intensified as her mum rambled, "It sounds like a fun day, doesn't it? What do you say? Are you going to spend it with us?"

Her eyes watered. Surely this wasn't over some boy? It must be because of the sun in her eyes. Her mum and dad waited for her answer, both their brows furrowed. How do you lie while looking in someone's face?

"I'm—I'm not," she stuttered before blustering through her lie. "I'm going to go swimming with Emma. That was an excellent idea of Dad's." Fluffy brown hair caught her eye, but she held her gasp inside and hid her grin as Chris stepped closer. Lucie shook her head briefly to force him to stop. "Aren't I, Emma?"

She stared at her, imploring her to join in with the lie.

Emma stood to her side, staring back, her brows furrowed in suspicion. Lucie blinked in Chris's direction. Surely all their years spent together had given them telepathic abilities.

But what if Emma chose not to support her? What if her dad grounded her and she never saw Chris again?

Panic gripped her heart as Emma eyeballed her.

Emma briefly looked to where Chris stood before returning to Lucie. Her eyes were wide in surprise. This was it. No moment mattered more than this. What would

Emma say?

"I'm swimming with you and Jess. Aren't I, Emma?" Lucie repeated, beseeching her.

Emma's silence was longer than the wait for a presenter on a reality show to announce its winner.

CHAPTER TWENTY-THREE

Was Emma ever going to speak?

Her future with Chris and maybe her entire happiness depended on her little sister. Lucie gritted her teeth and stared at her, silently begging her.

"Yeah, she is," Emma eventually replied, deadpan.

"Hold on. I know this was my idea, but you haven't got your costume," Lucie's dad grumbled as Lucie began to tremble. Chris was stepping closer again. "I guess you want the key. I suppose we can wait here while you run there and back. Maybe we can go and sit on the beach for a bit."

The pancake was climbing up Lucie's throat. How could her one lie catch her out instantly? She'd never be allowed to see Chris again or leave the lodge if her dad found out her plans.

Lucie desperately tried to communicate her need for support to Emma. How was she going to get out of this moment? Tears brimmed her eyes, but she clenched her fists, fighting against her body as it tried to betray her.

"I brought her costume with mine on the off chance she'd join us," "I brought her costume with mine on the off chance she'd join us," Emma said half-heartedly. Lucie could kiss her, even if her lie hadn't sounded wholly convincing.

It was enough, because her mum threaded her arm

through her dad's. "Come on, David, let's leave them to it. And don't forget, we've got to get to bowls, or we lose our deposit."

Her dad hesitated, but unsurprisingly the threat of losing money was the real catalyst, and soon they were rushing in the direction of the outdoor bowls with a shouted goodbye.

"Don't forget your special dinner," her dad added as he rushed away.

When he was gone, Lucie found Chris sharing a hint of a smile as he gave a tentative wave.

Lucie waved back sheepishly. Warmth spread across her chest, replacing the earlier ache. The butterflies were back too, and she didn't curse their presence, because she'd missed them.

"You're seriously lying to Dad and bringing me into it for a guy? And he's not just any guy, but the one I already warned you about. He has a reputation for a reason. You're so out of character right now, Lucie." Emma grunted.

Chris was close, but he didn't say anything. Instead, he waited patiently with hunched shoulders and his hands in his pockets.

"I thought you were better than this," Lucie said, letting her confidence rise. "Don't you dare judge him when you don't know him. I decided to lie, and he had nothing to do with it. He's not perfect, but neither are you or me, and our parents are so far beyond perfect, however hard they pretend in front of others." She pointed in the direction they'd gone.

Emma dropped her voice, her eyes softening as she shared a rare moment of vulnerability. "He's going to hurt you."

Lucie faked a smile and took a slow breath. "We're mates hanging out," Lucie whispered back. She wanted so much more from him. "Besides, isn't it time a guy broke my heart? I want to experience life, and that might mean making bad decisions and lying and getting into trouble. But isn't that what you wanted for my holiday and my eighteenth? Didn't you want me to live a little?"

Emma shrugged. "Stay safe, yeah?"

Lucie smiled. "Cross my heart."

Emma jumped at her, forcing her into a hug. "If you have anxiety issues, head back to our lodge. You'll be okay there, and Jess's parents left one of the keys hidden on the locked bike so you can get in if you need to."

"Thanks, Emma. I love you."

"Love you too," Emma replied before turning to glare at Chris. She walked away without a goodbye.

As Lucie looked at Chris, a squeal of excitement tried to force its way out of her mouth, but she squeezed her throat and faked a cough to keep it in.

Chris stared at her, fidgeting and shoving his toes into the sand repeatedly. Was he nervous?

A shiver crept up Lucie's arms. Prepared for the heat, she'd worn a T-shirt with shorts, but his presence gave her a chill. Chris came back for her. Her behaviour yesterday could have been enough to keep him away for good, but it hadn't.

Lucie took a deep breath and stepped closer to Chris. The softness in his eyes stopped her from running in the other direction.

"Hey," she said, relieved it hadn't come out as a croak.

"Hey," he replied. They stared at each other in silence. Birds tweeted from the trees, and the sun heated her bare arms, but his green eyes distracted her from everything else around them.

"I'm glad you're here," she said, reaching to yank on her ponytail before letting it fall through her fingers.

"I wasn't sure you wanted to see me again. I thought you'd tell me to get lost after yesterday. I'm sorry for pushing you about studying law at university." He fumbled with his rucksack strap.

"Don't apologise," she replied with a shrug of her shoulders. "I wanted to see you, and I'm kinda embarrassed by the way I reacted. I'm sorry too."

"You don't need to apologise. Wow, listen to us." He closed the gap between them, his smile growing. For a moment, they stared at each other. Jitters filled Lucie's belly, and she fought the temptation to lick her dry lips.

"Chris, I—" But what could she say?

"Yeah?"

Numerous questions tumbled through her consciousness, but she couldn't get them out. So instead, she squeaked, "Nothing. It's nothing."

"Oh, and happy birthday! That should have been the first thing I said." He slapped his forehead with his palm. "I got you a card and a present."

Her face heated quickly. Yesterday was quickly forgotten. It would be her first card from a guy she fancied. Was this a dream? "You didn't need to."

"I wanted to. The card is in my bag, but the present is an activity. But you don't have to do it if you don't want to, although it's going to be amazing. We've got to go now, or we'll be late. Do you trust me?" Chris asked quickly. He gave his rucksack another shove and held out his hand.

Lucie stared down at his hand. It was getting harder to predict which were good decisions and which were going to get her hurt. What did Chris have planned? Her belly jolted. She barely knew him. But he'd shown so much of himself and gifted her the confidence to try. She had to trust him, didn't she?

Be the exception.

She slipped her hand in his and let go of all the things that might stop her.

His dimples appeared, and his eyes sparkled.

CHAPTER TWENTY-FOUR

"**Y**ou want me to what?" Lucie shouted at a wincing Chris.

Branches swayed around them as birds squawked and children, hidden amongst the trees, shouted instructions to each other. But, apart from the sounds, the only hint that she and Chris weren't alone were the little orange helmets visible between green leaves as people of all ages tackled the high ropes course that made up one of the forest's activities. From below the trees, parents encouraged their children, and groups of friends shouted at each other while laughing and calling out their support.

Lucie and Chris had spent the last hour on these high ropes around the trees. She'd crossed rickety bridges and swung on ropes as her legs trembled and her hands shook. Then, when they'd walked across a taut rope with a second rope at hand height to steady them, she'd nearly shouted at him to get her down. Chris was there for every step. He'd held out his hand when she'd completed the series of planks that threatened to upend her and cheered her when she mastered the climbing wall. His smile and words of reassurance aided her in tackling each terrifying and new part of the course, but none of it compared to the final challenge. A 270-metre zip wire across the lake loomed in front of her. Her belly dropped, and tears brimmed in her eyes.

"I want you to go on the zip wire," Chris said, his voice getting quieter each time he spoke. "When I say I want you to, it's a suggestion. You should only do it if you're happy to."

"Happy?" It came out as an embarrassing screech.

"Sorry, that was the wrong word," he replied, blanching. He said each word softer than the last, as if he was trying to calm an angry tiger. "If you want to, not for any other reason."

Lucie's heartbeat was frantic. It was a choice. Chris wouldn't force her to do anything she wasn't comfortable with. She could climb down the ladder, and they'd never speak about it again. It was similar to when she had something she had to say, but fear stopped the words from coming out. When she didn't say what was in her heart, the memory of giving up and succumbing to anxiety seared her soul forever. She could do the zip wire, but the concept petrified her. The instructors were well trained, and the equipment was safe. Was it the heights, being out of control, or embarrassing herself that terrified her more? Fear stabbed at her confidence, puncturing it. Fear told her she was a chicken and that Chris would laugh at her or reject her if she didn't go through with it.

He was wincing.

Nearby, a couple of children that couldn't be more than ten got strapped up and then took on the threat of the zip wire with screams of laughter. They made it look easy. But it wasn't for Lucie. A couple a little older than them had already politely asked if they could slip in front. The instructor, who was preparing people to go, rolled her eyes. Lucie glanced again. It wasn't a roll of her eyes but an encouraging smile. She'd read that you wrongly perceived in others the adverse reaction you expected them to have when you had low self-esteem.

Why am I like this? I should believe in myself.

Why did the path of the zip wire have to be so high? The end, over the water and into the trees, was far away.

Lucie's head swam, and she closed her eyes to stop it, but that made it worse. It was like water was circling in her head, throwing it off balance. She attempted a deep breath, but it turned into an out of control wheeze. Was she going to have another anxiety attack? She couldn't get away from Chris now. By the time she made it to the bottom of the steps, it would be too late. She'd be hyperventilating. And what if she fainted in front of brave children and strangers? And then what would Chris think of her? Again, panic hit her chest, and she imagined having a heart attack on the ropes. Lucie opened her eyes to find the steps and saw the two people in front of them in the queue, getting strapped up in preparation for the zip wire. Her body shook, and she closed her eyes quickly again. Her eyelashes soaked up the tears that brimmed her eyes, although one got away and slowly fell down her cheek and rested on her upper lip.

"Talk to me, Lucie," Chris begged, his voice quiet beneath the fog of anxiety.

She opened her eyes and found his forehead marred with lines and his mouth small. Somehow, with her eyes open and staring at him, a little tightness eased. Leaves brushed her face as Chris took her hands and walked her, with tiny steps, away from the others to a quieter part of the large wooden platform.

"Breathe with me, Lucie." He ran his thumb around her wrist. It seemed to trick her pulse point into slowing a little. "You're going to be okay. Keep breathing. You're safe here with me. I'm not going anywhere, and I'm not going to leave you. We won't do this bit. Once you're ready, we can climb down the ladder and sit quietly. But don't worry about that now."

She shook her head aggressively. Strands of her hair slipped from beneath her safety helmet.

"No?" he asked, his brow furrowed. "Okay. When you're ready, tell me what you want to do. I'm happy to do whatever it is you want to do next. I do have a question though. My mum used to have panic attacks, and they were a bit like this. Is that what you're going through right now? Just nod. You don't need to speak if you can't."

"It's an anxiety attack," she said quickly between short breaths. "A bit different, but similar."

Chris nodded slowly. "Okay. Remember what I said to you about being the exception?"

Lucie nodded, her entire focus on Chris.

"I got it from Mum. She would say it to me when I struggled. It didn't always mean standing out from the crowd. Sometimes, when she said it, she meant taking care of herself and doing the boring routine stuff to stay healthy was being an exception. Many people don't listen to their bodies or push themselves until they break. Sometimes being the exception means being willing to take a step back and taking time to be self-aware."

He was speaking slowly with long pauses. Lucie was sure he was doing it for her benefit, but it was difficult to hear him against the rushing in her ears. Sickness threatened to rise from the pit of her stomach.

As if sensing a further escalation in her anxiety, he drew her attention again. "Lucie, look at me." His green eyes were wide, and a chink appeared in her panic. Briefly, she remembered staring into his beautiful green eyes when they were talking on the beach. "Can you repeat 'Be the exception' with me?"

She nodded again.

"Be the exception. Be the exception. Be the exception," Chris whispered as he stared into her eyes. Lucie joined in, and they said the words quietly together. He continued to run his thumb across her wrist as he held her hands. She focused on the words and allowed them to wash over her.

"What else can I do to support you?" he asked so gently it hurt her heart.

"This is good," she replied breathlessly, focusing on how his mouth moved when he spoke. Her heartbeat slowed, and the tightness eased.

"There's something else my mum taught me that we did when she had attacks. But tell me to shut up or shake your head if it's not helping," he said tentatively. He raised one eyebrow, and his mouth was tight as if he was straining to keep everything under control. "Tell me five things you see."

The unusual request threw her for a moment. Lucie hesitated.

"Five things you can see, Lucie. What can you see?" he asked softly.

She looked wildly around her, desperately trying to avoid the water. "You, zip wire, blue skies, ropes, trees," she replied, breathlessly stuttering through the words.

"Well done. How about four things you can feel?"

She took a deep breath, focusing on everything against her body. "My harness against my chest, my helmet, your finger on my wrist and—" A clicking sound distracted her as the instructor attached a karabiner to the last person's harness.

"Stay with me. One more thing you can feel." Chris stamped his feet, offering a hint.

"The boards under our feet. I can feel the boards," Lucie said, letting out a breath of relief.

"You worked out my subtle hint." Chris smiled. "Okay, now tell me three things you can hear."

The fog in her head was clearing, and the rushing in her ears wasn't as intense. She closed her eyes and let her other senses take precedence. There were lots of different noises, and she could distinguish between them. Usually, during an anxiety attack, it was a wall of sound. Maybe it was easing. "Birds, there are lots of them. The instructor is giving instructions to the person they've clicked in, and I can also hear some kids shouting. They sound happy," she finished. Lucie opened her eyes and offered him a brief smile.

"How about two things you can smell?" Chris was smiling back at her.

"I smell green, which makes no sense, but whatever it is, it smells green, probably the trees. Oh, and I can smell Lynx."

Chris blushed. "Finally." He let go of one hand and shoved his hand in his pocket before bringing out some mints. He flipped a polo into her free hand. "Tell me one thing you can taste."

Lucie popped it into her mouth, twisting it around with her tongue. The ridges of the mint pressed against the roof of her mouth before she stuck the tip of her tongue through the hole. "I can taste mint."

He flipped one into his mouth and said with muffled speech, "Me too."

They smiled as they sucked and munched on the little peppermints. Tiredness crept over Lucie, which was a typical response after an attack, but there was something else this time: freedom, now she'd got through it. Although she always got to the other side of one, tiredness and shame usually accompanied the experience. But this time, it was different. The techniques offered her hope. Beyond Emma holding her hand and making her breathe, she didn't know there was a way to lessen the avalanche of a full-blown attack, but she could use the technique Chris showed her again. Maybe there were other activities out there too. Was it time to speak to her mum about getting help rather than hiding the problem away?

"Thank you," she said, holding his hand. It was warm and clammy, but she didn't want to let go, not ever. She liked him more than that morning. Chris helped her rather than laugh at her attack or ditch her. "I normally run away when an attack is coming, but I'm trapped here."

She said it as a joke, but he saw straight through her defence mechanism.

"Do you get anxiety attacks a lot? Is that what happened yesterday outside the coffee shop?" He asked the question, but she was sure he already knew the answer.

Lucie chased the dissipating mint around her mouth with her tongue. This attack had made her vulnerable, but sharing this weakness was a choice. She fumbled through her words, attempting to reply without making the difficult situation more embarrassing.

"Lucie, it would be helpful for me to know in case it happens again," he explained.

The expectation that she had to share brought anger

rising like a ball in her throat. "It won't."

"It's happened twice in twenty-four hours."

"Because I'm scared, okay?" she said, raising her voice. "They've been escalating since I've had to talk about school and university more."

"I made you do this, and I made you talk about university yesterday." His face softened, and he dropped his head. "And now I'm demanding answers from you when, if I remember right from mum's attacks, you should probably sit down and eat something as you must be exhausted. They used to take so much out of her."

She was tired and tetchy. It wasn't just the attack that made her angry. It was opening up to someone she still had questions about. Chris held her close, but she was sure it was because he was scared that she might collapse from a lack of energy.

"I can help you down via the steps. It shouldn't be too tricky together. I should have asked before planning something like this. I wouldn't have booked this activity." His guilt made her squeeze his hand tighter.

"Please don't apologise. I've never told anyone other than Emma. I'm scared of so much, including how you'll react. I'm waiting for you to walk away from me," Lucie said, allowing herself to open up a little.

"Why would I?"

Telling him the truth was scarier than jumping into the sky with a bit of wire holding her up, so instead, Lucie took a deep breath and focused on the path of the zip wire. She gulped noisily. The line stretched across the expanse of the lake before disappearing beneath the trees. It had to be safe, but that didn't make it more attractive. What about the bike ride the day before? She was terrified at the top of the hill, but she'd ridden down it anyway and loved every thrilling second. She couldn't keep missing out on life because of her fears. "Can we talk about it later? I don't want to go down the steps. I want to go on the zip wire. I think I'm ready."

Lucie gripped his hand, unable to hide her fear completely, and walked closer to the instructor before he could stop her or question her motives. "We're ready to do the zip wire."

Her heart thudded, and there was a tremble in her legs that she couldn't hide, but it was the good version of fear, like at the top of the hill. It was as if her body was excited, not terrified.

"Okay," the instructor replied. "Which one of you is going first?"

Chapter Twenty-Five

With one last wary look at Lucie, Chris grabbed the zip-wire rope and jumped off the board.

As gravity carried him farther away, he turned in her direction. He was too far in the distance for her to recognise any facial expressions, but she imagined the thoughts running through his mind, as they were probably the same ones going through hers.

She'd encouraged Chris to go first because she needed longer to compose herself. With Chris, she'd gained so much, but she refused to do something just to impress a guy, even one like him. It had to be for her. It was time to prove to her dad, the girls at school, and everyone else who'd doubted her who she was. Maybe if she could do this, then she'd have the confidence to talk to her dad about art college and talk to Chris about how she felt about him. After all, what was scarier than letting go while jumping off a high-up wooden platform?

"Are you ready?" the instructor asked.

"Already? He's been gone for like ten seconds!" Lucie exclaimed. "Sorry, I didn't mean to shout that."

"It's okay, you're allowed to shout," the instructor joked. She beckoned Lucie forward and attached the clips and ropes. "It's been five minutes."

"Oh," Lucie blushed. "I'm a bit nervous."

She expected sarcasm from the instructor, but instead, the instructor leaned in and said, "I get nervous when I do it, and I've been on this zip wire hundreds of times. It's supposed to be a bit frightening, because if it weren't, then the rush wouldn't be as huge. It's a good kind of stress. Trust me when I say that you're going to love it."

Up until this weekend, Lucie hadn't trusted anyone except her family. But meeting Chris, trying all these new experiences, and then how Jess's parents spoke to her that morning was changing her. There were many good people in the world if she allowed herself to be open to them.

"I hope so," Lucie said, the expanse of sky in front of her.

"And if you don't, then you can find me and shout at me," she joked. "I'm Asha, by the way."

Lucie laughed as she stepped closer. Asha needed to prepare her for the jump. "Nice to meet you. I'm Lucie."

Lucie appreciated the way Asha explained what every clip and strap did. It helped alleviate some of her nerves, although she continued to shake. Vomit climbed up to her throat with each clink of metal.

"And your boyfriend will be waiting for you at the bottom. So if you get scared, close your eyes and imagine him cheering you on," Asha added.

Chris wasn't her boyfriend, but she didn't correct her. The idea that he was at the bottom, hollering in celebration, was a great motivation.

All the safety equipment was in place, and there was nothing else to delay the jump. Lucie stood on the edge and listened to Asha's last instructions.

"Ready when you are," she said.

Lucie swallowed nervously. Chris had helped her

across the ropes course, and he was worried about her as he jumped off the board.

You can do this.

Be the exception, Lucie.

She took a deep breath, closed her eyes, and jumped.

Air escaped from between her lips as gravity took her. It was slow at first. Why had she been so nervous? But it wasn't long before she gathered speed, and tentatively, she opened her eyes and marvelled at the blue sky surrounding her. It may have been daytime, but at her height, she imagined reaching for the stars. Maybe it was time to change the world too. She giggled to herself.

Hanging from the wire, she found herself turning 180 degrees. Where she'd jumped from appeared far away. It was as if she was staring back at the past version of herself from before this weekend. She gave it a little wave and laughed.

The wind chilled her ears, and she pulled up her legs to stop from catching the trees with her feet. She flew past the fir trees that she'd had no chance of touching and giggled. The water was calm from up here, and for a moment, the ripples from canoe paddles transfixed her. Then, she spotted the pancake house and where she and Chris had the sand incident. It wasn't a full two days ago, and yet so much had happened.

Metal slid across metal. The swing of Lucie's legs made her dizzy, but she kept her eyes open, refusing to miss any part of the journey. The wire took her past the activities beach with yellow and red canoes lined up. A group of teenagers on boats shouted hello as she flew over them. She called hello back, realising that they were the same gang she'd been scared of on the beach on Friday. A bird soared in the distance.

Trees surrounded her again, and she bounced slightly on the zip wire.

"Yeah!" she hollered as the end board and the second instructor came into view. Cheers echoed around her as she neared the end. She quickly turned. Chris jumped up and down, his arms waving in the air.

Was that it? It had been so quick, and she nearly demanded that they go on it again. Within seconds, the instructor grabbed her rope and dragged her to the end of the line, where Chris waited patiently. Her cheeks, cold from the wind, were suddenly burning. Chris grinned so wide at her that his dimples were the deepest she'd ever seen.

As the new instructor undid her clips and ropes, she and Chris stared at each other. Lucie's face displayed the same grin. Thrills of excitement covered her skin.

"You can go," the instructor said as soon as he'd finished, and she ran into Chris's arms. They jumped up and down and cheered together. It was a messy embrace with neither remaining still due to the adrenaline and excitement.

"You're incredible, Lucie. I'm so proud of you," Chris shouted.

"I was the exception," she replied and hugged him harder.

Chapter Twenty-Six

"I can't believe we did it!" Lucie shouted, throwing her head back.

They sat on the edge of the beach, tucking into the snacks Chris brought as a birthday treat. High above them, legs waggled, and strangers screamed as they took their turn on the zip wire that Lucie and Chris had enjoyed hours earlier.

Each time someone zipped down, a hint of the rush she'd experienced tickled her belly. Finally, she'd conquered her fears and taken the jump.

"You're amazing, Lucie," Chris said, his dimples showing as he stared at her.

Lucie shrugged as she bit into her apple, but she couldn't hide her joy, and a grin covered her lips as she crunched through the usually tart-tasting Braeburn. It tasted sweeter than she remembered. Everything was different. Was it due to conquering the zip wire or because she'd admitted her anxiety attack and got through it? Or was it Chris? Maybe it was because she wasn't scared of everything anymore.

The teenagers from the first day walked past, joking and shoving each other.

"Thank you for shouting hello earlier. It made me smile so much," she called out to them.

"That was you on the zip wire? Oh my god, you looked so cool," the oldest girl replied.

"Thanks," Lucie replied, wiping her apple juice–covered hands on her shorts. "It was a lot of fun."

"Were you scared?" one of the guys asked.

"A little," she said with a shrug. "I was petrified before I went on, but then when I was in the sky, it was incredible. You should totally do it."

"I couldn't. What if I fell off or vomited?" one of the guys said, and his friends nudged him and laughed.

"What if you never do it, and then you regret it forever?" she replied. "I wouldn't have done it without Chris." She was surprised at the intensity with which Chris stared at her. Hairs rose on the back of her neck, and she fought the temptation to hold his hand. As if reading her mind, Chris held out his hand, and she took it.

"Maybe I should do it," the youngest lad piped up. The group turned to him with their mouths open. He was the one they'd been burying in the sand on Friday. Had they presumed he wasn't confident enough to make the jump? "If someone came with me."

"I will," one of the girls said. "Let's go before we chicken out."

They headed off quickly before shouting their goodbyes and thank yous.

Lucie and Chris waved their goodbyes as they ate the last bites of their apples to the background noise of birds and lapping water. A comfortable silence descended between Lucie and Chris as they ate through the snack bars, sandwiches, and crisps that Chris brought.

It was tricky to eat and keep holding hands, but they didn't break them.

"What was scarier, telling me about your anxiety attack or the zip wire?" Chris asked, scooting closer.

Lucie smiled. "I can think of something scarier."

"Yeah?"

Lucie couldn't look at him. She needed to ask the question before she chickened out. "Do you want to meet up again after this weekend?"

He stared at her. "Yeah, I really do. That was one of the reasons why I wanted to learn about your attacks. I want to see you again and make sure I don't do anything to make them worse," he said slowly. She did look at him then, out of the corner of her eye. He turned to the water, and their thighs touched as she stared into the water too.

"When do you start uni?" she asked.

"In two weeks. Why?" he asked as he turned too and grabbed her other hand.

They sat cross-legged on the sand, holding hands. Chris's smile was tentative, and even as the sun heated her skin, a shiver crossed her belly. "Because although I'm back at school this week and studying non-stop, I can get away next weekend. We could meet up."

His tentative smile grew like a flower blooming for the first time. "Yeah, for real? There's a really cool café near the train station."

"The rainforest one?" Lucie blurted out. "With catcalling monkey sounds?"

"Yes! How do you know it? No one knows it. I'm surprised it's still open."

"I love it there. I try to get there once a month. I studied there in the build-up to my exams to escape home. If I tell you a secret, will you promise not to tell anyone else?"

"Yeah, of course," he replied. His eyes sparkled, and

197

she was reminded of his energy.

She leant closer and whispered in his ear as if they were in danger of being overheard. The scent of Lynx filled her chest, and she closed her eyes to savour it before speaking. "If you sit in the booth in the corner around lunchtime, rainbows appear on the table. I don't know how, because I can't see any prisms or anything, but they appear every time."

"Seriously?" he whispered back. "We have to meet there at lunchtime next weekend so that you can show me these rainbows."

His lips brushed her ear. Her legs trembled, and heat rushed through her stomach as his breath crossed her neck. They were so close. Should she ask him to kiss her? How did you know when the time was right?

"Tell me three positive things about you," he suddenly requested, inadvertently causing her to lean back to look at him.

She didn't hesitate in her reply. "I conquered several fears, I didn't freak out over the attack, and I spoke to those teenagers that I was scared of on Friday without overthinking it first. And one for luck, I'm happy."

He clapped his hands. "Yes, you are!"

"Your turn," she pointed at him animatedly.

"No one ever asks me. It's a tricky question to answer, isn't it?" he joked, pausing. "Okay, I can do this. Mine are that I give great presents, I'm kind, and I'm happy too."

Her chest was bursting with joy. "You give the best presents. I can't thank you enough for today. And thank you for the way you dealt with my attack too."

"No worries. I don't want to make it all about me, but working with you to get through that helped me too. I've never told anyone about Mum's attacks before."

She squeezed his hands between hers. "You can tell me anything, right?" They'd shared so much since they'd met. The one secret she still kept from him was that she wanted to kiss him, and that probably wasn't the secret she hoped it was.

"Okay. I trust you, Lucie. I really do. But this is hard to share."

"That's okay." Lucie wasn't entirely sure why she did it, but she turned around so that her back was against his chest. Maybe if he wasn't looking at her, he could say it. It took some awkward shifting, which destroyed any chance of romance, but soon she rested between his legs. The heat of his body was against her. Would it make her sweaty? It was worth it.

He held her close as he spoke. "The thing is, when I was younger, I thought that my mum left because I didn't have the skills to help her when she had attacks. As far as I knew, she only had them when I was around. I couldn't help her on her down days either."

He paused as families played nearby in the water.

"My counselling helped me to understand Mum a bit better, but I didn't say anything about the attacks. I was ashamed that I'd failed Mum and that people would blame me for her leaving. It's not that simple, but I still believe it on my worst days." The pain in his words broke her heart.

"Chris, no," Lucie jumped in. "Do you get how much it helped me to have you with me during my attack? It's the same when Emma does it. It's not about anything you do or say, although that was great. But having someone close during the spiralling thoughts means everything."

"For real?"

"For real. Do you know what? I reckon it helped your

mum too. You being there for her, even when you were so young and didn't fully understand, would have helped her. And not just during the attack, but after too. She wasn't alone. Please don't ever underestimate that or blame yourself." Lucie took his hands and held them between her own. "Do you miss her?"

"I miss what I remember. I feel guilty because I saw what she did to Dad and how he continues to suffer. But she was my mum. She had problems, but she was also a lot of fun." He laughed, catching her off guard.

"What is it?"

"Sorry, I remembered this one time she took me to the park when Dad was at work. More than once, she took me there, and I'd be wearing pyjamas. Dad would have hit the roof if he knew." Chris chuckled. His chest vibrated against her. "Sometimes, we'd pretend to be pirates hunting for treasure, or dinosaurs, or my favourite game was when I was a spaceman going to the moon and meeting an alien for the first time. Of course, she was always the alien."

"No way?"

"Yeah, she had this green mask that she'd made from card, and she'd wear it and chase me around the park. Those were the good days." His delight disappeared, and sadness filled the edges of his words.

"But there were bad days too?" Lucie asked tentatively, holding his hands tighter.

"Yeah, she had those too. They were horrible. But even with everything that's happened, I wish I could see her one more time and ask her why she left, but I guess some wishes don't come true." Chris faltered. Although his hands didn't leave hers, his shoulder bobbed. Was he wiping a tear away? "I just want to hug her one more time and tell her that I love her."

Lucie squeezed his hands to reassure him. "Your mum was lucky to have you, and she'd be proud of you if she met you now," Lucie replied. She let go of his hands, turning around and giving him a long hug. She didn't know what to say but hoped a hug would help.

Eventually, she turned back and drew his hands against her again.

"I wish your dad knew how lucky he was. Sorry if I shouldn't say that, but you're amazing. Everything about you is incredible, and he should tell you that every day," Chris said. Lucie's eyes were watery now too. No one had ever said that about her. Her dad made her believe she was a burden. She would never match his expectations but battled to do so even though it hurt her when he made digs or suggested she was a failure.

"Sometimes, I wish I didn't have to see my dad every day. It sounds mean because you don't get to spend time with your mum, but who would I be if I didn't carry the guilt of not being enough or the anxiety from trying to be the person he wants me to be? I used to say it to Mum, but she told me that we're fortunate we have him paying the bills and keeping a roof over our heads." Tears fell down her cheeks now, but she wasn't embarrassed to be crying in front of Chris. On the contrary, it was a relief to say the words aloud. Her dad should have been better. He was lucky to have her and Emma.

"Your dad and my mum were different. It's good that you can say stuff. You deserve a dad who loves you for who you are. From everything you've said, he should be shouting how proud he is of you. You work hard, are talented, and care about people. You're the best, Lucie.

You did a zip wire, for goodness sake."

Chris held her close, and they both cried through the pain of their family situations. It was freeing to share with someone how she felt about her dad. It was only that morning Lucie was willing to admit it to herself. But telling someone else was scary. He could have told her she was ungrateful or an ugly person. She was fortunate to have a roof over her head and do all the activities they did because of money, and she didn't take it for granted. But she longed for a dad who told her he loved her or was proud of her. Instead, her dad opened his mouth to remind her of her failings. Emma endured it too, but as a result, she'd developed the energy to live life as she wanted.

Lucie caught the chatter from a family getting ready to go on the inflatable water challenge. The children excitedly asked questions about what would happen if they fell in and if they would get cold in their wetsuits. They were scared the water monsters would bite them and hurt them.

"The water monsters are friendly and will take care of you until we get you. And you have a special vest, which means you can't go underneath," one dad said as he picked up his son and tickled him. "I wouldn't let anything happen to you." They were so happy. Why had she never had that sort of relationship with her dad?

"Sorry for bringing the mood down," Chris said after a while.

She puffed out air as if in a brief laugh. "You didn't. You gave me a chance to be me. I will never be able to thank you enough for that. And you were right in what you said about yesterday. An anxiety attack was coming on. I ran away because I'd never had them in front of anyone but Emma, well there was kinda a time in front of dad too.

Normally I message Emma and ask her to help me, but I haven't got my phone, and neither has she. I had to get away from you. I didn't want you to see that I'm messed up."

"You're not messed up," he replied, and she turned to look at him. He squinted against the sunlight reflecting off the water.

"No, but I should be doing something about the attacks. It's because of Emma's research that I learnt they're called anxiety attacks, not panic attacks. I've been too scared to look into them, but I should ask Mum or school for support after everything today. Maybe I can't stop the attacks, but if I learn ways to calm myself or reduce them, then I won't be so scared. And I won't run away from people like I did yesterday."

"I'm glad I didn't scare you off for good." He smiled before suddenly bobbing up and down like he had ants in his pants. "Oh, and the day isn't over yet. For a start, I haven't given you your card. I don't have any other activities planned, but we could walk through the forest. What time do you have to be back?"

"I have a birthday dinner at five tonight, so I should go at quarter past four to get ready. I can't be late. I'll be in so much trouble if I am. Like walking over hot coals, locked in the cupboard under the stairs levels of trouble," Lucie joked.

Chris checked his watch. "Okay, we've got two hours. I'll set a timer on my phone." He dragged his bag closer and reached into it. "Here's your card, by the way."

He placed a thick white envelope into her hand. He stared at her with raised eyebrows and wide eyes as she slipped her finger through the paper and ripped it.

Bright reds and yellows caught her attention as she

pulled the card free.

The words "I bet you thought I bought you a birthday present..." were accompanied by the image of a cat with a massive head and huge open smile.

She opened the card gingerly. As she opened it, the sound of laughter exploded. It was a card that played noises.

The non-stop chuckling made her smile. Inside, the message read, "Of course not!"

"Sorry," Chris said. "They didn't have many options in the shop here. Read the bit I wrote on the back."

She turned it over and smiled at the scrawl. Chris wasn't like any guy she'd met before, except when it came to his writing style.

To Lucie, I'm so glad I met you. You've made this the best weekend ever, and I hope you'll visit me at university one weekend. Love, Chris.

Lucie felt the familiar blush creep onto her face. She nodded excitedly. "I'd love to visit you."

"Really? That's the best news ever!" Chris jumped up and fist-pumped the air. He wriggled his bum in glee, making her giggle. "Right, let's go and discover more of this place. But before we do, I want to hear the card laugh again."

Lucie opened the card, and they laughed at the chuckling coming from the birthday card. They were probably weird to anyone nearby, but Lucie didn't care. She was happy, and she didn't want to hide it.

CHAPTER TWENTY-SEVEN

They'd been talking for what felt like hours, but the timer hadn't gone off yet. The best thing about the holiday village was that when you slipped away from the hustle of the activity area, there was no one else around. The skinny jean mums with generic buggies and bearded husbands swarmed the main buildings. In the depths of the forest, where little lodges popped up around them, they were free.

As they walked hand in hand beneath the canopy of trees, they shared their most embarrassing stories. Chris talked of getting so drunk that he didn't know what he was doing at his leavers' ball and woke up on the golf course in the middle of someone's round. Lucie fell off stage while singing in the school musical. Chris tried not to laugh at that one, but his chuckles behind his hand quickly turned into bent-over belly laughs when she'd joined in. It was funny, yet it was the first time she'd laughed about the experience. Usually, shame covered her, but it was okay with Chris by her side.

Even in the heat of the day, his hand was comfortable in hers. There were times it got a bit sweaty, and they took a second to wipe their palms on their shorts, but immediately they'd reach for each other and continue their walk.

How would she be able to say goodbye to him? What if he got to university and met someone and they fell in love? Lucie's stomach tightened, and she held her breath. Chris wasn't her boyfriend, and they'd just met. But she wasn't special and couldn't compete with all the girls at his university.

Beams of sunlight found holes between the branches, and at times it was as if they were walking through a mystical world where no one else existed. Within this moment, they were free from family dramas and education stresses. She breathed in the flowery fern scene that surrounded them.

A squirrel bounded across their path before clambering up one of the oak trees by the side of the road. It was two days ago when the family car stopped by Chris and those squirrels argued like her dad and his. It was too much to let herself hope they would meet next weekend at the café. What if her dad found out? He'd never let her date a boy, especially not during term time when she should be spending every moment studying and especially not Chris.

"What are you thinking about?" he asked.

She shrugged. "What it will be like when we get home."

"I won't forget you," he said as they reached a clearing near the back of some lodges. How did he know it was worrying her? He dropped his bag down, and Lucie caught a glimpse of the sweat patch on his back. It was gross, but she didn't care.

Would she have to touch his back if she kissed him, or should she hold him somewhere else? She tried to recall episodes of her favourite teen drama.

"Will you forget me?" he asked tentatively.

"Never," she whispered, surprised at her honesty.

He grinned back at her. "Good, although I won't let you. I can't wait to show you around Manchester. I'll find the art gallery where there are some awesome paintings and drawings, and we can go and visit loads of places that will inspire your art. Of course, we'll have to go for a fancy dinner and enjoy the local pubs and visit every part of the city. The cool places and the geeky ones."

"At this rate, I'll have to stay for a week," she joked.

"You could stay for half term. I'd help with your university application, and you'd be able to do homework while I attend lectures." Chris's dimples were showing, and his shoulders bounced in excitement.

Did he really mean it? Her dad wouldn't let her, but the possibility of a week with him made her giddy. She wanted to bounce her shoulders in time with his.

"I need your number first though," he said casually, but with his lips sucked into his mouth and eyebrows raised, he appeared vulnerable. Suddenly Lucie remembered that he'd written his number on the drawing she'd binned during the anxiety attack. How had she forgotten? She couldn't ask for it again because then he might be annoyed that she'd binned her drawing of him. Lucie worried her lip with her teeth. "If you want. I mean, I don't need to have it."

"I didn't get it last night because I didn't really think you'd meet me today, but as soon as I get back for my birthday dinner, I will ask for it so I can give you my number, I promise," she said quickly. It sounded like she was lying, but she wasn't. He looked up, and she held his gaze as if trying to convince him.

"Okay, because I can't contact you without it. I like

207

you, Lucie. Would it be okay for me to follow you on Facebook?" he asked with an awkward laugh and a wince.

Shit. Chris would see how geeky she was and how few friends she had if he went on there. "I don't really use it," she lied.

"Okay," he replied with a shrug. But his dimples disappeared, and his hand was limp in hers.

"But I've thought about joining Instagram to see other artists and show my art. So I could open an account and follow you on that. Do you have Instagram?" She fumbled through the words.

"I could get it. I'll join tonight while you have your birthday dinner and then tell you my handle. How's that?" Chris asked with a fresh giddiness to his words.

Lucie beamed. "That would be amazing."

"Awesome." The dimples flashed back on his face, and he squeezed her hand. "I wanted to tell you something."

She held her breath.

Suddenly a song carried on the breeze. Together they gazed at the nearest lodge, where a window was open. Lucie recognised it as one of the songs her mum sometimes played, "Hold You in My Arms" by Ray LaMontagne, who was known for his folk-rock sound.

Through the lodge's lounge window, they witnessed an elderly couple dancing to the song. The white-haired man was bent as if time hadn't been kind to his body, but he continued to hold the lady's hand, with his other hand on her back. Their cheeks touched as they swayed to the music. Occasionally, the couple would move their heads to stare at each other, and the man would mouth the words of the song to his love. Even at their slow speed and hunched stance, it was evident by the tenderness on display that they were in love.

"I want to be in love like that when I'm older," Chris uttered softly. "They look so happy."

"Yeah, same," Lucie said so quietly the sound barely carried over the song. "You'll have to learn to dance first though, if you want love like that."

"Who said I can't dance now?" He held out his hand to her. "Miss Lucie, if you would do me the honour?"

Heat filled her cheeks as she took his hand in hers. Her legs shook as he wrapped his arms around her neck, and she wrapped hers around his waist. Standing under the trees in the holiday village, she was about to dance with a guy. She'd never been to any of the balls the school publicised with the local boy's college, only the discos when she was twelve. Chris's body was warm against hers, and at their proximity, she smelt a mixture of his musky scent and Lynx. She breathed him in and melted into his arms as he guided them from side to side.

It was getting harder to swallow as she gazed back at him. Flecks of black swam in the green of his eyes. She couldn't look away, and she didn't want to.

"You know," he whispered into her ear. Goose pimples rose on her arms. "I had a cheesy thought when I saw those people dancing. Maybe I made it up or read it in a book. But I reckon that although life changes us, nothing changes us more than falling in love."

"I've never been in love before."

"Me neither. Well, I hadn't." Did he mean he was in love now? Her dreamer side held tightly onto those words, wishing them to be true. "But no matter what happens in life when you fall in love, your soul keeps that person safe in your hearts, and no matter where you go and what happens, you carry their imprint for the rest of your lives."

Chris was unlike anyone she'd met before. He played the fool and made her laugh, but when he spoke seriously, he had a way of reaching her heart and making everything okay.

"Whenever we fall in love? Are you sure?" The way her heart raced at the idea of kissing him and the fear of never seeing him again—this was like love, wasn't it?

Should she try and kiss him now? She was too scared to make the first move, but what if the timer went off and she had to go home for her birthday tea? She had to kiss him now, or she'd be too frightened to try again.

"Well, not if we fall in love with arseholes. They can bugger off. They don't get a place on our soul."

The tension from the moment ceased, and a chuckle broke free. But at the same time, relief and shame combined inside her. Why were all her emotions so heightened? She wanted to shout, cry, and belly laugh all at once. Would she always be too scared to kiss him?

"Oh, I forgot, let's go somewhere quieter," he said, breaking contact and retrieving his bag. "I have one last thing for your birthday."

Was it going to be another funny card? Was he unaware of what nearly happened? He was going to give her another jokey thing when the moment was perfect for a kiss. They walked away from the lodges, the elderly couple now forgotten, and into a quieter bit of the forest.

They reached a small open area and stopped. Chris kept his back to her as he knelt on the floor with his bag. She moved to the side, but he hunched down, hiding what he was doing. Then, like a lunchbox opening, a popping sound filled the area, followed by the flick of a lighter. As he turned and stood, delight replaced her confusion.

"A birthday cake with a candle for me?"

"A birthday cupcake. But it's all yours. You don't have to share it, although not knowing what your favourite flavour was, I picked mine instead, because who doesn't love chocolate? But you don't have to share it if you don't want to." He was so earnest in his hunger for the cake that she giggled aloud. He frowned before adding, "You'd best blow it out before the candle melts. And don't forget to make a wish."

She closed her eyes, took a breath, and blew out the candle.

I wish to have my first kiss with Chris.

She couldn't deny him some of the cake, and they took turns taking big bites out of the chocolate sponge. It was gone in a matter of seconds. Buttercream covered his upper lip, and she struggled not to stare as he licked it off. Her belly spun like a washing machine.

"What did you wish for?" he asked.

His eyes transfixed her. Should she say? It might not come true if she did, or was that an old wives' tale? The ball of fear grew inside her. She had one chance. The timer must be about to go off. This was it. Time to be the exception and make her wishes come true.

She took a deep breath and dived for his lips, banging his head and squishing his nose but never reaching his mouth.

"Ouch," she exclaimed as he rubbed his head. She waited for him to laugh at her or freak out and tell her they were friends and nothing more.

"I've wanted to kiss you all day, but I didn't know how you felt. That wasn't how I imagined it," he joked, sending pearls of excitement flying around her body. "How about this instead?"

He cupped her face with his trembling hands and planted a kiss on her lips. Initially, it was the fumbling kiss of novices. The butterflies in her stomach were doing belly flops. Adrenaline roared through her ears. Where should she be putting her hands? Little tickles crossed her neck, and it was like pins and needles were attacking her legs, and yet, even with all that going on, it was bliss. How could you enjoy something that was like torture? His tongue eased open her mouth. It should have been weird to have someone else's tongue in her mouth, but it made her fancy him more. The smell of Lynx filled her lungs as his eyelashes fluttered on her skin. He tasted of buttercream and chocolate cake. There was so much going on. She shouted at herself to enjoy the moment. Then, as her thoughts slowly eased, a ringing bell replaced the sound of their kiss.

They pulled back and gasped for breath.

"That was—"

"Amazing," she finished for him.

"I was going to say the best kiss ever, but I like amazing too!"

Her smile was as broad as his, and she couldn't stop giggling.

"But you've got to go to your birthday dinner," he reminded her. Thank goodness for his rational side, as she would have carried on doing that the entire day. "But I'll see you tonight after?"

"Yes, I can be on the beach at about seven thirty." She was breathless as she turned around to get her bearings. Where were they? She had to go, but she didn't want to leave him. They were farther from her lodge than she'd realised, and she needed to get back. But they'd meet later and kiss loads more. The day wasn't over yet.

"You promise? You'll definitely be on the beach at exactly seven-thirty?" He chewed his lip as she walked away. It was fun to tease him, but she wouldn't forget to come back to him.

She turned back. "No matter what," she replied.

His dimples were on show, and his green eyes were sparkling. "And don't forget to bring your number."

She giggled again. "Hmmm, I'm not sure I can give it to just anyone."

He laughed back. "Please, please. I'll join Instagram too. I can't wait for you to visit me at uni."

She ran back to him and pecked him on the lips before running back down the path to her lodge. She turned around as she jogged; Chris was standing in the same position, staring at her with a smile. The sooner she went, the sooner she'd be back to kiss him some more. Lucie waved and hurried on, brushing a thumb across her smiling lips and giggling.

CHAPTER TWENTY-EIGHT

Plates clattered as her mum cleared the last of the cake from Steve and Jacky. Lucie swiped a look at her watch. Quarter past seven. If she sprinted, she'd be at the beach in time. It would be close, but it was doable. She flicked her bangs and slowly counted to ten.

Dinner was chaos. She'd been on the brink of an incident the whole time due to her drifting attention. Occasionally Emma glanced suspiciously in her direction. Lucie's ears burnt on and off throughout the birthday song and cake cutting. Usually, it was because everyone was staring at her, but she feared they were reading her this time.

She wanted to kiss Chris again. Maybe she could ask him to be her boyfriend tonight. But she needed to leave right now. The words burnt her tongue, and she couldn't keep them in any longer. She'd been polite and attempted conversation, but she had to go right now.

She cleared her throat and stood. "Thank you so much for my birthday dinner. That cake was the best, and everyone was so lovely. Can I leave the table now? There's somewhere I need to be, and I need my phone too, not to send messages but to check the number."

"No, you may not leave the table, and you are certainly not having your phone," her dad replied angrily.

"But—"

"You have been rude this entire time. Your mum worked for hours on this, we are sitting here with guests, and you have been checking your watch and fiddling with your hands this entire time."

"But I—" she attempted to get a word in, but her dad wasn't listening. Lucie fidgeted with her hair. Her face was burning. "Dad, I—"

"You've barely spoken to anyone, grunting when asked questions about your application for your law degree. The least you can do is wash up, but not before you've had my permission to leave the table. I'm ashamed of your behaviour."

Emma rolled her eyes and huffed loudly, but it wasn't her battle. But how could Lucie stand up for herself if he wouldn't let her get a word in?

"I'm sorry, Steve and Jacky, for the way my obnoxious child has insulted you." Of course he was making a point in front of his friends.

"I hadn't realised I'd been so rude." Anger sliced through her tone of voice. "I can do the washing up when I'm back, but I need to go now."

He raised his voice. "What you need to do is sit back down." He was always trying to control her, like he tried to control everyone else.

I wanted just one night.

Emma stood up too, but she sat back down at a shaking head from their mum, although she still grunted and glared at their dad.

"I will not sit—"

"You will do as I say, yo—"

"Let me talk," Lucie shouted. Emma gasped, and Jess covered her giggling mouth. "For once in my life, let me talk rather than making us listen to you. All you do is tell us what we should do and how we should behave and that we should listen to you. But you never listen to us."

"Lucie, please calm down," her mum said softly.

"No, I won't. I have to go out," she pleaded.

"Why?" Her dad stood and faced her. There was an edge to the atmosphere, but no one else spoke.

"What?" Lucie grunted.

"Why do you have to go out? What is so important that you want to ruin your birthday with your family? What can be so crucial that you would shout at your dad, who has paid for you to have a relaxing holiday before you go back to school?"

"I—" Lucie stuttered, remembering what had been said about Chris before. If she told them, they would laugh at her, and Emma might not talk to her again.

"Tell me, Lucie." Her dad locked eyes with her as he spoke slowly. "What is so important that you would ruin this entire holiday for? You wanted to speak, so speak."

Lucie gulped a breath. She raised her voice so that she was louder than he'd been. "I have a friend I need to meet right now."

"That boy from earlier? If he is the reason for you disrespecting me, then I'm glad you're not seeing him tonight, and you will not be giving him your phone number. Today is your special birthday, and you are ruining it. You will enjoy the rest of your birthday with your family. And don't you dare shout at me again." He stared her dead in the eyes.

Her breathing was rapid, and she clenched her fists to stop from lashing out. "You can't stop me. I am eighteen."

"Don't try me, Lucie. I can stop you if I have to."

Tears ran down her cheeks. She'd never thrown a tantrum before, but she wanted to now. Why couldn't he understand how important this was to her? She had to see Chris.

She reached for her glass, desperate to calm down, but her hands shook so violently that she knocked it instead, spilling water everywhere.

"That's it. Get to your room. You've spoilt this day for everyone. It should have been a happy occasion, but your behaviour has ruined it. You're grounded for weeks. No going out unless it's for school and then straight home after. Now get out of my sight!"

She bolted upstairs. Tears rolled down her cheeks, and she fell onto her bed, sobbing. The wetness from her face quickly soaked through her pillow, her sadness a mark on the cover. Chris was a good guy; every moment they'd spent together proved that. She had to get to him. They wouldn't meet at the café because she was grounded, and she couldn't contact him to tell him.

Rain pelted the window, reflecting her mood. Summer rain was violent and consuming, and tonight was no different.

It was like the tears wouldn't stop as she shook against the duvet. Stabs of pain plunged into her belly, and she wanted to wail against the world. She'd never felt agony like this before.

Footsteps out in the corridor made her raise her head. Had her dad come upstairs to shout at her again?

The soft rap of knuckles on her door told her that it wasn't him.

"Sweetheart, can I come in?" Her mum's gentle voice made her cry harder.

She sobbed a yes before she buried her head back in

her pillow. The bed depressed when her mum sat down. Suddenly, there was a hand stroking her hair. Her mum hadn't done that in years. When she was younger and her dad made her cry about silly things, her mum would pop her on her lap and stroke her hair, telling her that he didn't mean what he said. She always apologised for him, but it never made it okay. He never apologised for anything.

Lucie's tears continued to flow, nearly drowning out her mum's voice. "I'm sorry he scolded you, honey. He shouldn't have done that, but it's because he cares. Maybe he shouted like that because he's not used to you answering him back or because Steve and Jacky are here," she said, the softness in her voice no doubt an attempt to soothe the situation.

"Don't make excuses for him," Lucie replied, her voice muffled by the duvet. "And don't make out this as my fault."

She'd never spoken to her mum like that before. Lucie always ensured she was on her side because her dad wasn't, but she refused to make allowances for his behaviour this time.

"You're right. The way he acted was wrong, and this is his fault. I'm sorry, honey." Noises of the television downstairs reached Lucie's bedroom. "Come here, Lucie. Let me hold you like I used to. I haven't hugged you in a long time."

Lucie climbed onto her mum's lap. She was too big for it now, but it was nice to be held by her mum again. She rocked Lucie gently. Her mum was soft and smelt of hand soap. It was the same as when she was younger.

But I'm different now.

"Mum," Lucie whispered, as if saying the words too

loud would make her dad come upstairs and shout. "What am I going to do? I love him. Can you fall in love in two days?"

Her mum didn't laugh or call her an idiot. Instead, she was quiet for a moment, and then she said something Lucy never expected. "You can fall in love instantly with the right person."

"You fell in love instantly with dad?" Lucie struggled to hide her surprise.

"No, I met someone before your dad. I fell in love with him the moment he said my name. He came over with his school to spend time with Uncle Mike's drama class with a French exchange programme. He made me laugh all the time. I've never told anyone this because it sounds silly now, but when we kissed, it was like fireworks."

"Really?" Lucie stared at her mum, who was lost in her thoughts.

"I know, it doesn't sound like me. Maybe it was a blip, because we lost touch when he returned to France. After that, I met your dad when I was working in a café before university. Then life happened, and before I knew it, I was pregnant with you."

Lucie knew from things her grandma had said that her mum's pregnancy was quick and unexpected. "You were eighteen, my age when you had me." The tears had stopped falling, although occasionally Lucie hiccupped and a sob came out.

Her mum sighed. "Yes. I had all these plans for university, but your dad's career was more important than my education."

"I'm surprised he was okay with you having a baby."

Her mum stuttered. "He wasn't initially. But that's another story. He had a lot of girlfriends before me, and I suppose I was the lucky one that he settled down with."

The revelations were falling fast from her mum. "Do you ever think about the French guy?"

"Alain? I did for a while, but having two girls under five meant I was busy enough. Alain friend requested me on Facebook the other day, but I was worried about your dad seeing that I'd added him. Your dad ignored me for a couple of days when I added one of the guys from work. I had a good snoop on Alain's page though." Her mum went quiet again, and the banging from downstairs replaced the silence. Then suddenly it was a lot quieter there too. "You shouldn't miss your chance though. You should meet with that boy."

"Chris?"

"Yes, Chris." Her mum pushed a piece of paper in her hand. "Here is your phone number. Your dad won't know. I'll find a way for you to look at your phone even though you're grounded. I told your dad to go out for a drink with Steve and Jacky. They're going to keep him busy so that you don't need to worry about him. I encouraged him to make the most of his last night. I'm sorry I didn't defend you earlier, Lucie. I promise I will do better next time. Make sure you avoid the route to the main complex so that you don't bump into your dad."

Lucie grabbed the number and pecked a kiss on her mum's cheek. Lucie's eyes were sore. She saw her reflection briefly in the mirror. They were swollen and red from crying too, but she didn't have time to worry about that. She had to meet Chris. Hopefully, he waited for her. He'd understand once she told him everything.

She ran downstairs and caught a glimpse of Emma and Jess as she flew through the living room area.

Lucie threw herself through the door, and headed for the road but a hand grabbed at her.

She turned to find Emma. She must have jumped out the house after her. Emma stood in the pouring rain, barefoot in just joggers and a hoody. She swiped at tears as she met Lucie's stare. "I'm sorry, Lucie. I'm so sorry."

Lucie stuttered, but words wouldn't come out.

"I was horrible to Chris. I'm the worst sister." Sobs shook her body as Lucie pulled her back under the porch. Lucie needed to get to Chris, but the vulnerability across her sister's face made her heart ache. "I don't understand why I've been acting so bratty. But you really like him, don't you?

Lucie nodded. "He's funny and stupid and really fit. And he makes me feel like I don't need to be scared to be me anymore. I want to be his girlfriend. Have you ever liked someone like that?"

Emma turned to the doorway but quickly turned back to Lucie. "Yeah, I guess. But more importantly, I love this side of you. You were amazing when you stood up to dad. I couldn't look away. Do you forgive me?" Emma moved from foot to foot and looked to the concrete floor.

Lucie yanked her into a hug that filled her with an instant warmth. "Whatever happens with Chris, it's still you and me. I love you, Emma. And you're allowed one mistake," she whispered in her ear.

Emma beamed back at her. "I love you like Dec loves Ant."

"And Ant loves Dec," Lucie replied. Everything was forgiven, and their sisterly love and friendship was back on track. Emma pushed Lucie into the rain, and she bolted down the road in the summer storm.

Emma shouted, "Thank you for being the best big

sister in the world. Go get your man!" It was like something out of one of their mum's television shows. Lucie laughed as Emma gave her a double fist pump. Her words carried as far as Lucie before dying in the wind.

This was it. Her whole future was based on this moment. She was going to get her man.

CHAPTER TWENTY-NINE

Heavy rain beat down on her as she sprinted down the path towards the beach. Droplets of water bounced off the ground as she dodged the puddles. The sound of the rain hitting the trees and crashing into leaves made the moment appear mystical, but she didn't have time to stop and listen. Strands of her fringe stuck to her face, and the rain poured down her cheeks. It dripped off the trees, landing in big globs of water around her.

She checked her watch. It was five to eight, and she wasn't close. Inside lodges, families celebrated their last night before returning home. Laughter and loud conversations pushed through the sound of the downpour, but she continued running without glancing further at them. Her dress, a pink cotton thing she'd borrowed from Jess to wear for dinner, and her meet up with Chris, clung to her legs. It was soaked through and made it tricky to run. Her thighs burnt from the speed. The stone path was slippery in places, and for a second, she imagined slipping and breaking her leg.

Be the exception.

Her heartbeat was rapid, and her chest ached from breathing in the air now chilled from the rain. If she stopped for one second, she'd sob again. But she didn't have time to cry. She had to get to Chris. Lucie blinked rapidly to clear the drops that settled in her eyelashes as she attempted to get her bearings, but the driving rain that showed no signs of stopping made it impossible to hear or see where she was. She paused briefly on the path and searched for a sign. Suddenly someone pushed her from behind, nearly shoving her into the bushes. Lucie gripped the phone number in her hand tighter. She couldn't lose it.

"Why would you stop in the path, you silly girl?" an angry woman holding the hand of a small child said. Her glowering face peeked out from under the hood of her yellow raincoat. Lucy shrunk under her stare.

"I'm really sorry," Lucie stuttered as she rubbed her now sore shoulder. "I didn't think. I—"

"No, you didn't think. You're another one of those selfish teenagers," the stranger replied. "Maybe you should think about others rather than what you want." But Lucie wasn't selfish, and the woman hadn't needed to walk into her. There was plenty of path. Lucie's teeth scrapped at her bottom lip. She should tell her that, but instead she listened, her head slumped, as the woman continued her lecture. After Lucie apologised several more times, the woman finally dragged her child away to the nearest lodge.

A tear slipped down Lucie's cheek. Would she ever be free of her fear at speaking up? Chris had helped her so much, but it wasn't enough.

Lucie shook herself. She needed to get to Chris. Her promise to meet him filled her heart as she began to run again. She hit a puddle with a splash, and muddy water jumped up and covered her legs. What would he think of her arriving in such a state? That was if he was there. He had to be there. She must keep believing it.

Lucie reached for the hem of her skirt with her left

hand and gripped it tightly. She was faster now that it wasn't around her knees. She clutched the phone number her mum gave her tightly in her right hand. Her hand ached, but she wouldn't let the piece of paper go.

Lucie ducked her head to stop the rain from clouding her vision. Tears brimmed in her eyes, but she didn't have a hand free to brush them away. A car horn beeped behind her. Were people leaving early? Lucie jumped out the way and headed down another path, desperately searching for a quicker route.

The trees surrounding the beach came into view. Lucie stumbled as she glanced at her watch. It was already eight o'clock. If Lucie had spoken up to the woman lecturing her, would she have arrived sooner?

Please be there.

She ran onto the beach, nearly toppling forward at the change in surface. The space was empty. Gasping for air, she ran to every part of the beach, but she couldn't find Chris. She dropped her dress and pushed her lank fringe out of her eyes. Maybe he'd hidden under a tree or the nearby water sports roof to get out of the rain.

It will be okay.

But it was too late.

"Chris," she called out. Her voice was hoarse. He wouldn't have gone without saying goodbye. He would have waited. Why hadn't he waited?

Her search was fruitless. Chris wasn't there. Maybe he'd never come in the first place. Had the whole weekend been a trick or a game? No, it couldn't be. He'd meant the things he'd said.

Maybe he was ill in bed or he'd hurt himself. She had to get to his lodge. If Lucie followed the paths, she'd find the place where her dad had stopped on Friday. Was that two days ago? She'd find him and explain everything. If Chris were annoyed that she'd stood him up, he'd have to forgive her once she shared the truth.

Lucie ran through the resort, freezing when she got to the holiday village pub. Her dad sat in the window, and she ducked down in case he could sense her even in the darkness. He laughed with Jess's parents as if he didn't have a care in the world. Lucie hesitated briefly as she stared at him. Was she wrong to be doing all this for a boy? Maybe he was right. She should be focusing on her studies and not trying to meet up with Chris. Her dad was older and wiser than her. Maybe he did know better. Should she give up? Lucie remembered the things Chris had said about his family and his future. He trusted her with that. It had to mean something, didn't it? Lucie shook herself before continuing. All the things Chris had told her meant something to her.

Her running was slower now. Her dress was limp and dripping, and her trainers sloshed with every step.

It was harder to find her way to his lodge in the dark and rain. Every section and building were the same. The rain slowly cleared, leaving a cold mist that settled on her skin and made her shiver. Tears threatened to fall down her cheeks, but she refused to cry. Crying wasn't going to solve it. She had to find his lodge.

Lucie ran for what felt like hours. Her limbs got tired, and she shook from the drop in adrenaline as she found new paths and corners she didn't recognise. Her breath was like a brief fog in front of her as she panted in the now quiet forest. Shadows loomed in the darkness from gaps in the trees, and the occasional movement made her move faster. A branch scratched her legs. She was lost. Water continued to drip from where it settled on leaves in the storm. It hit her cheeks before running down and merging with the aftermath of her tears.

"Be the exception," she shouted to the trees, refusing to give up. She had to get to Chris. Panic hit her chest, but she kept it at bay. How did a conversation about studying law make her feel like she might die and yet being scared and alone in a forest didn't bring on an anxiety attack?

Clinking bottles caught her attention. She'd found the road with the lodges on it again. She passed people ditching their rubbish and recycling with a bang and clatter as she trudged down the road, breaking into a light jog when she recognised his road. She glanced at her watch and saw it flash five past nine.

It would be okay. She would explain everything. The light in the living room of his lodge through the darkness drew her to the window. She stared through the glass, hoping to catch a glimpse of him or his dad.

She gasped and held her chest. The tears fell liberally then. She cried loudly and hugged herself tightly as the sobs threatened to explode out of her body. Her heart hurt more than it had in any panic attack.

He was gone. There was no one in the lodge. They must have forgotten to turn out the light as they left.

She had no way of contacting him, and she'd never see him again.

She slid down his door, and her head slumped against her chest. Lucie wept loudly as the piece of damp paper with her number on slipped from her hand and floated to the wet ground.

CHAPTER THIRTY

PRESENT DAY

"I refused to talk to dad for a month after that day. When I did speak to him, it was to say that I wasn't studying law at university anymore. Instead, I intended to study art and travel the world," Lucie finished.

Chris had returned with their drinks before she'd gone through the events of the last evening. His face was so animated during her story that she'd struggled not to laugh, even at the sad bits.

"What did your dad say when you told him that?" he asked. His eyes were wide as she shared her revelation. "He must have been livid."

Lucie laughed. It hadn't been funny at the time, but so much had changed since then. Everything with Chris was the catalyst she needed to reach for her dreams and stop trying to please a man who would never be happy except when he was telling her what was wrong with her. "Dad threatened to cut me off, but I'd been saving money from every birthday and my weekend jobs. I had money to get me started, and over that month, I'd researched scholarships and other opportunities. I wasn't going to let him destroy my dreams. I was always going to be the exception."

His smile made her ears tingle. Was he proud of her?

"Something unexpected happened too. During the argument about me attending university, Mum stood up to Dad. She told him that she had money saved and would contribute whatever was needed. Then Emma said she had enough saved from making jewellery for her friends and their friends. She would give it all if it meant I was following my dreams."

Chris's laugh was loud, and her smile was uncontrollable as she spoke. "Emma was a little entrepreneur. We all underestimated her in those days. Now she's a massive success. She has a couple of retro jewellery boutiques and a booming online store. She continues travelling the world with her wife when she can. They live in Australia with their baby, and they're opening a new boutique while enjoying the sights. I can't wait to meet my niece."

"Bloody hell, I've missed a lot. But you have to tell me." He leaned in. "What happened with your dad after?"

"That was the biggest surprise. That weekend changed all of us. Before Christmas, Mum left him. She said she'd stayed with him for us, but after that weekend, she realised that he did more harm than good." Lucie sighed. That year eased the pain and sadness that had lived inside her for years. "Mum and I talked about my anxiety attacks too. She ensured I got the best help. Unfortunately, she carried a lot of guilt about those attacks and blamed herself for years. It wasn't her fault. Living with Dad for so long destroyed her confidence and self-belief."

Lucie wished she could go back and tell herself that it would all be okay and that she didn't need to be scared of everything.

"Wow. I don't know what to say," Chris uttered.

"You'll never guess what my mum is doing now. She's getting ready to move to America with her new husband, who she met online. They were in a forum for parents of children with anxiety attacks. They fell in love, and he moved to the UK to work for a company in Birmingham to be close to her. Now they want him back at their head office in California, so he's taking Mum with him. She's happier than I thought possible. Sometimes, I catch her berating herself or reliving some horrible stuff Dad had said to her. But when she does, I make her tell me three positive things about herself. She used to struggle with two, but she can think of lots now." Chris grinned back at her. Did he realise the impact he'd had on her entire family? That Chris was a teacher now, inspiring hundreds of kids, couldn't be more perfect. The students were lucky to have him. "I don't speak to Dad anymore. Every time I tried, I came away feeling like a worse version of myself, so I cut him out of my life."

Chris took her hand. "I'm so proud of you, Lucie. You've surpassed every dream I had for you. I wish I'd known you during that time."

She took a deep breath and held him tight. "You have to tell me. What happened to you that last night? Did you come to meet me? I considered that you might not have wanted to meet me. I'd never kissed a guy before and wasn't sure if I'd done it right. I presumed you'd pitied me."

"That kiss was amazing, and I'm as sure now as I was then it was the best kiss ever! I got there early that night." He was nodding emphatically as he spoke. "I thought maybe you'd changed your mind. I thought you might have hated the kiss or not fancied me anymore, or maybe you didn't want to be around me again. I cursed myself for being so full-on about you visiting me at university. I waited around for a while, but I was on a deadline because of a family emergency. When you went home to your birthday tea and I got back to the lodge, my dad told me my grandma was ill. After a heated debate, Dad let me stay around long enough to say goodbye to you. But when you didn't come, I presumed you'd changed your mind. He picked me up from the beach before eight, and we drove straight home. We must have just missed each other."

"And was your gran okay?"

He blushed. "I love that that is your first thought. Yes, Gran was fine. Nothing gets to her. She probably has these medical crises to keep us on our toes. She has the strength of an ox. Seriously, I'm not joking. That eighty-year-old woman beats me in an arm wrestle every time."

Lucie grinned.

"I was too scared to search for you online. I thought if I got in contact, you'd reject me. Also, Lucie Smith and Emma Smith are common names. I did search for you a couple of times," he confessed.

"Chris Jones isn't that unusual either," she joked back.

"I waited for you at the café a week later like we agreed," Chris added. It wasn't an accusation but a request for information. His voice dropped, weighted by the sadness that filled his words. "But you never came."

"I was grounded for weeks. Even though I refused to speak to him, Dad wouldn't let me out of his sight. But eventually we had that big argument, and everything changed. As soon as I could, I went to the café. I sat in the Rainbow café most days after school and on weekends on the off chance I'd see you, but you'd gone to university by then."

"I went to the café every day before university. I sat and waited in case you came, even though I believed you'd made your decision and decided you didn't want me. I was upset, but I couldn't forget you. I presumed you agreed with your dad and had returned to your life of working towards university to study law."

"No way? We probably kept that café going for a couple of months. I eventually found you on Instagram, even with your generic name. You were having the best time at university, and I realised I'd missed my chance. Once we moved, I didn't come back here and didn't bother trying to contact you. The self-conscious negative version of me won over and told me you never really fancied me anyway."

"I did though," he added, his green eyes still fixed on her. "I really did. You were everything. I never forgot you."

"I never forgot you either." They stared at each other. She held her breath. Should she make the next move?

The memory of Bradley suddenly hit her. She couldn't do anything until she'd spoken to him. It was unfair on all of them. She ran her tongue around the inside of her mouth, contemplating her next words, when a familiar tune caught her attention. The first bars of "Hold Me in Your Arms" by Ray LaMontagne played from the pub's speakers.

"That's not a coincidence?" she asked, her head tight from the intensity of her furrowed brow.

"I queued it on the jukebox when I got our drinks. I hoped it would play in time," Chris said, his dimples showing.

She beamed back. He hadn't forgotten their song.

"I played it every day for weeks," he admitted. "Eventually my university housemates told me that if I didn't stop playing it, they would destroy all my electronics. So I got headphones. I listen to it once a month now."

She held her phone up to show him her favourites on Spotify. "I listen to it regularly too."

"Do you want to dance?" he asked, standing and holding out his hand.

She skimmed the patrons. It was a mixture of students getting cheap meals and wizened men nursing their pints.

Be the exception.

"Sure." She took his hand, and they swayed to the tune, oblivious to everyone else in the pub. It was as if they were back in the forest, lost in the moment when she'd wanted him to kiss her. Only now, they weren't awkward teenagers but two changed adults.

The familiar shivers skittered down her arms, and the butterflies flew around her belly. She breathed him in, wondering if he had any Lynx left in a drawer somewhere. Her head was light, and her thoughts of the past disappeared. The heat from his hand against her back made her body thrum. Lucie closed her eyes and stroked the nape of his neck with her fingertips before letting the music guide them. The notes of the song she'd had on repeat after that weekend carried her through emotions until she was back in his arms in that forest, hoping for a future with the boy with the beautiful green eyes and dimples when he smiled. She wasn't sure if it was the memory of first love or that they were something special to each other. But she couldn't let him leave again without taking his number. She needed to give them a chance.

"You never did give me your number," he whispered in her ear, as if reading her mind. His cheek was warm against hers, and she sighed happily.

"I'll have to check with my mum first. I can't be giving out my number to just any guy," she replied, smiling.

"Not even one with dimples like these and wearing a fantastic suit?"

She giggled. "When you put it like that." His fingers traced her chin. Her heart whispered that adult Chris was someone she could love. Now was the time to tell him her true feelings, no matter the consequences.

Lucie took a deep breath and opened her mouth.

"Babe!" Bradley's voice called out from the other side of the pub.

CHAPTER THIRTY-ONE

Lucie and Chris broke apart from their dance. Guilt washed over her face. She should have finished with Bradley sooner, but she might have missed Chris if she had. Had fate stopped her from getting the train and finally given them their lucky moment? It didn't matter because Bradley was making a beeline for them.

"Sorry," she said quietly as Bradley walked to them. He quickly dived in for a weird mixture of hug and handshake.

"Babe, we need to talk."

A rush of adrenaline roared through her ears as she blurted, "It's over, Bradley."

Bradley stared at her and shrugged.

She took his hands as she scolded herself for making this situation more awkward than it needed to be. "I'm sorry, Bradley. I shouldn't have said it like that. I've enjoyed our time together, but we're not right for each other. You know? And I don't want to be in an open relationship." Chris's presence behind her was distracting, but she shook her head and focused on Bradley.

"Yeah, that's okay. I don't think we want the same things, and you never seemed that into me. We were just passing time with each other, weren't we?" Lucie froze. Where was this side of Bradley before? Had her behaviour been that obvious to him when even she hadn't realised that's what she was doing? "And thanks for ending it. I've wanted to do it for a few weeks but didn't have the guts."

Lucie smiled as her phone began to ring. That had been much easier than expected, even though she'd shouted it was over after being caught dancing with another guy.

"But I want to be friends, yeah?"

"Yeah," Lucie replied, giving him a brief hug as she flicked the button to answer the call from the Bristol number. She witnessed Bradley introducing himself to Chris from the corner of her eye. She nearly giggled when he tried to high-five him, and Chris jumped back like he was going to get a slap. "Sorry?"

"This is Jen at Morphosis. Is that Lucie Smith?" It was her interviewer.

"Yeah. I mean, yes, this is Lucie."

She mouthed to the guys that she needed to take the call as she grabbed her bag and moved outside into a quiet corner of the beer garden. There were a couple of smokers discussing politics, but other than that, she was alone.

"It was great to meet you today," Jen explained. The familiar brush-off. "We've finished all the interviews, and yours was by far the best. Your presentation on how you would run the project we gave you blew us away. We love your ideas, your creativity, and your passion. We're delighted to offer you the job."

"I'm sorry. Could you repeat that last bit, please?" Her throat was suddenly dry, and sweat beaded the back of her neck.

"We'd like to offer you the job. You were fantastic, and you can do great things with us. You can have a day to—"

"I don't need a day. It is a massive yes. I've dreamt of working for Morphosis for years. I studied you at university and knew even then that I wanted to be on the team. I accept." Lucie shimmied in the corner of the pub garden in a celebration dance.

Jen laughed down the phone. "That is the best news. We'll be in touch next week with a contract and information about your start date. In the meantime, go and enjoy your weekend. We can't wait until you are part of the company. I can't tell you how excited I am that you will be joining my team."

"Me too, and thank you." Lucie held her squeal of delight until she'd hung up the phone. Her dream job at her dream company!

The first person she wanted to tell was Chris and then Emma. He was barely back in her life, and yet he was already the one she wanted to share her news with.

She ran back into the pub to find Bradley waiting for her at the bar.

"Your mate had to go, said he had to catch his train or he would miss the wedding or something." Bradley shrugged. "You want a drink?"

She shook her head as the blood rushed from her face. She'd lost him again. She'd had the best news in the world followed by the one thing that would ruin everything. Chris hadn't said where he lived in Bristol or what school he worked at. It had to be easier to find him now, but hadn't she read in an article that lots of teachers didn't join social media because of the students?

Slowly she thumbed her tattoo, desperately searching for a bit of logic to fix the situation. She wanted to cry and shout, but instead, she closed her eyes and forced back the tears brimming at her eyes.

"Oh," Bradley said, dragging her attention back to him. "He told me to tell you that he left something on the table for you."

"Thanks," she exclaimed before bolting back to the table. A piece of white paper caught her eye. It was from the art pad she'd bought when she was seventeen years old. On it was her shooting star and a phone number. She smiled. It also held the drawing she'd completed of Chris on the beach eight years earlier. At Chris's scrawled message, she held her breath, willing herself not to get her hopes up. But the butterflies that had resurrected in her belly refused to listen to her naysaying.

Lucie, meeting you changed my life eight years ago, and I never forgot you. I couldn't bear the thought of never seeing you again. It hurt enough before because I don't think I ever stopped loving you. Please keep in touch, Chris

Her heart swelled as she stroked a fingertip across the drawing of the boy with the beautiful green eyes and dimples when he smiled.

"Babe, who was that guy to you?" Bradley asked, knocking into her, his beer sloshing over the number on the paper. "Oh, crap, sorry."

He grabbed some napkins and dabbed at it, but the number was smudged a little. She made out most of the numbers. There were several combinations she could try to get hold of him. But what if something happened and they missed their moment again? She stared at the image of him that she'd drawn.

Her hands trembled as their weekend from eight years

ago flashed through her mind. The moment their eyes first met, the faces Chris made as she drew him, the confidence he'd given her when she'd asked for chocolate chips, the honesty they'd shared, and the way they'd flown together down the hill on their bikes. The images came faster as she got closer to that moment of being in his arms as they danced before her first proper kiss. That weekend had changed her life in so many ways. What if she never got the chance to be that person again?

I have to see him.

CHAPTER THIRTY-TWO

"**W**hat am I doing here?" Lucie whispered to herself from the corner of the pub. The phone number was blurring even more because of her dabbing. If she ran, maybe she could reach the train and say goodbye properly. She had to have her moment.

"You need to run to see that hearts tie, Chris guy," Bradley said.

"Yes. I do." Lucie's eyes widened. When did Bradley get astute? Maybe they could be friends because she liked this side of him. She searched for her stuff, but she already had it all. This was not the time to fluster but to be decisive. Lucie kissed him on the cheek as if she was kissing goodbye to her old relationships and readying herself for something new.

"I'll call ya," Bradley said in her ear.

"Please do."

She ran through the pub, dodging chairs and avoiding bags people left on the floor. Emma's shout from the forest repeated in her ears. I need to go get my man.

Lucie gripped the drawing tightly in her hand. Whatever happened, she wasn't losing this paper that Chris had kept safe all this time.

Lucie dashed across the walkway and ran to the station, thanking no one in particular that she didn't need to elbow her way through crowds. Her Mary Jane heels and swishing skirt were not ideal for the panicked run, but she kept going, fighting the demons from her past that told her she couldn't have what she wanted. Nothing was going to stop her from getting to the station.

Concrete and glass loomed in front of her, and she ran headfirst at the electronic doors that opened at the last minute. She squeezed through the gap and continued her pursuit of happiness.

It was like she was back at the holiday village on that Sunday night, bolting through the rain, desperate to get to the beach. She didn't carry the same fear as she had that night. Something different gripped her belly this time.

Announcements surrounded her, and she caught a whiff of coffee and perfume. Where was he? It was as if she refused to let her eighteen-year-old self fail. That Sunday night, sobbing through the holiday village was one of the worst moments of her life, and if she could go back now, she would have told her eighteen-year-old self that she would do everything to make it okay. Life was going to work out. Was this run her way of telling herself that?

She suddenly stopped in front of the screens that announced which platform each train was on by final destination. It made no sense to be rushing to Chris like this. His train must have gone by now, but she had to try to get to him. She scanned the screens. What was the final destination of the train or what time it should have gone?

She touched her eyes, expecting them to be wet with tears, but there was nothing. Was it because she'd hadn't given up hope yet? It wasn't over.

"Excuse me," she shouted boldly to a guard several metres away. Strangers stared, but she barely saw them. "What platform for the train to Manchester?"

"Manchester? That would be platform five, but it's—"

She ran to the stairs that led to platform five, shouting a thank you behind her. She didn't want to hear that the train had gone. She wasn't losing her opportunity to say goodbye. Not this time.

Suddenly she saw the same grey-haired stranger who'd ploughed into her after her call with Emma before she nearly had an anxiety attack. She shouldn't stop, but all the realisations she'd had about herself from being with Chris again forced her to say something. "Hey, you. You banged into me earlier and didn't apologise."

The guy looked startled as he fumbled his words. "I expect you walked into me."

"No, I didn't. If I had more time, I'd sit you down and talk to you about appropriate phone behaviour and respect, but I have a heart to win. Just don't do it again, okay?" Lucie refused to move until he agreed even though she knew how imperative time was.

"Okay, sorry." The stranger shrugged, but his attitude wasn't the most important thing that second.

"Good," Lucie shouted before reaching the staircase.

Her heels clicked noisily as she took two stairs at a time. There was a train a couple of platforms away. That had to be platform five. Maybe she'd make it to wave or mouth goodbye and get his number again before it left. She ducked past a mum trying her best to juggle her toddler and their Peppa Pig backpack. Lucie smiled as she continued her mission. It didn't matter what challenges were going to get in her way. She'd reach ~~him.~~Chris. Lucie needed to believe that.

A man who looked like Lucie's dad stood in her way, and she stopped for a moment doing a double-take before ducking past him too. Instead of the shame that normally catapulted through her when she saw someone who looked like him, she felt ambivalence. It was like she was running for her future and all these diversions were easy-to-win challenges.

A shrill whistle sounded.

"No, no, no," she shouted.

Lucie ran across the bridge before sprinting down the next set of stairs as desperation gripped her heart. As she looked up, a greying old train eased from the platform. It increased its speed as it left the station. He was gone.

"No," she shouted as she continued down the stairs. Sadness gripped her. She apologised to the eighteen-year-old girl who'd wept outside an empty lodge eight years ago. Luck was rarely her friend, but she thought this time she would have a chance. Maybe getting her dream job was all the luck she was allowed.

She fell to a bench and unfolded the piece of paper and stared at the drawing of Chris. Those dimples got her every time. The numbers were smudged more now. The first six were kind of straightforward, but then they blurred from the beer. Was that an eight or a three? The last two numbers were illegible.

Her heart beat rapidly, and she filled her lungs to get her breath back. They'd lost their moment again. Losing Chris again was like losing a part of herself. Her heart was like concrete in her chest, and she debated whether she'd made more of it than it was. Maybe the universe was telling them they weren't meant to be more than ships that passed in the night.

Lucie paused and stared at the image she'd drawn of him in the holiday village, realisation dawning on her. Maybe meeting Chris was the reminder she'd needed to show her how far she'd come since they first met. Maybe they'd never meet again, but she hadn't failed. Instead, she found herself. Stopping to duck around the man who looked like her dad and telling the stranger off had slowed her down, but those brief moments meant something. They reminded her who she was now and who she could be if she remembered to be the exception. She never wanted to lose that confidence again. Lucie gave the drawing a soft smile and a silent thank you as she folded it back up and gripped it tightly in her hand. The realisation didn't stop her from wanting to tell Chris she'd always loved him or giving their future a chance though. But sometimes destiny wasn't on your side.

"Lucie?"

She turned to find Chris smiling at her. His eyes twinkled, and his smile was broad enough to make her stomach flip.

"My train was delayed. That last one was holding it back, but it should be here in a couple of minutes. I would have stayed in the pub waiting for you if I'd known I had a bit more time. Did you run to see me?" he asked.

She thought back to that moment when she'd jumped off the wooden board and hung on to the handle of the zip wire. That was the most terrifying moment of her life, and yet as her fingers trembled and goose pimples covered her skin, she now felt the same combination of fear and thrill. She glanced briefly at the hearts dotting his tie and smiled.

"Yeah, it's silly." She swallowed noisily and took a quick breath. "But I had to tell you I never stopped loving you either."

Chris quickly crossed the short gap between them. He cupped her cheek, and his lips brushed hers. "I didn't want to leave the pub earlier. The thought of not getting your number caused me physical pain. Lucie Smith, you're the best thing that's ever happened to me."

Her heart exploded in her chest as he kissed her again. His hand was hot against her face, and her body trembled as chills crisscrossed against the back of her neck. He was tender, and the softness of his lips made her skin tingle. His hand slid to the back of her neck, and the kiss deepened. She nearly giggled at the idea of easing her tongue between his lips. It was like their first kiss, but with something extra. The hope of the future? The roar of a train accompanied their kiss that now had the heat of adulthood and the sweetness of first love.

They broke apart, and she smiled as his tongue lingered on his lower lip. He grinned, and she knew a blush was covering her cheeks. He spoke carefully. "This is reckless, but do you want to come to a wedding? You could buy a ticket on the train, and you are dressed beautifully. I'd love for Dad to meet you properly, and I'm not ready to say goodbye now that we've found each other again."

Lucie rubbed her thumb over her tattoo. She wouldn't start her new job for a couple of weeks, and house hunting could wait. She didn't want to say goodbye or "keep in touch."

She nodded quickly. "Be the exception," she replied with a smile and was rewarded with sparkling green eyes and the deepest dimples she'd ever seen.

"You're the exception I can't be without," he replied. His lips brushed hers as she gripped the paper in one hand and whispered to her teenage self that there was hope.

He took her empty hand, and they walked towards the train as the butterflies that had lain dormant for eight years fluttered in her belly.

Acknowledgements

I'm incredibly lucky to be surrounded by supportive people who check-in, listen to my stories and share them too. Thank you, Asha, Gill, Kaz, Kells, and many others.

Many notable authors have helped me with this book through their beta reading, including Sarah Smith, JL Peridot, and Mark J. These authors have helped me develop my writing and find motivation to release books. Sarah helped when I considered the direction to go in with this book. I am eternally grateful to her. A massive thank you to Kathryn Kincaid, the brilliant author of the ice hockey romance Play Your Part and creator of worlds I can't get enough of. She's supportive and knowledgeable. And when I don't think writing is for me, she pulls me up and gets me through.

A big thank you to Joanne Machin, an editor I will always be grateful to because of her patience with my words. Her changes and comments are always helpful and considered, and they also help me learn and develop.

Thank you also to Avery of AveryDaisyBookDesign, who

made this beautiful cover and made all my visual dreams come true. She's the best.

Keep in Touch was personal for a variety of reasons. I've suffered from anxiety throughout my life and yet, like many, presumed that I'm problematic, hard work, and need to "get over it". Support from a counsellor at a tough time in my life and my recent ADHD diagnosis has helped me in ways I can't explain. But others have listened, offered support and ensured I never felt alone. When I started having anxiety attacks, I wasn't sure where to turn, but again, I had the best people around me who gave me hope, and I'm indebted to them. Through these people and other medical and mental health professionals, I've also learned about self-soothe bags, grounding yourself, and the techniques that can help when everything feels overwhelming.

I don't usually talk about my day job, but I wouldn't have written this book without it. In my work, people I support open their hearts and share their stories with me. Their willingness to do that has enabled me to tell my stories and share the importance of support and having someone who may not always understand you but is still there for you, celebrating your successes and staying close when there are challenges.

Thank you to the lovely staff at the pub where I write. They share their lives with me, have my order ready when I arrive, and never suggest I overstay my welcome. Unbeknown to them, they motivate me through my secret hobby.

Finally, I want to thank (the fictional) Pacey Witter. He was my first love and the inspiration for this and many stories. He's the ultimate first love.

ALSO BY REBECCA CHASE

SPICY ROMANCE BOOKS

Head Over Feels: Sexy and funny debut contemporary romance

Stalling in Love: A steamy opposites attract romance

About Rebecca Chase

Rebecca Chase is an English rose and a pocket rocket with a taste for drama, romance, and love. She adores writing, whether it's a short story with unexpected passion or a novel that takes you through the ups and downs of a blossoming relationship. She's always looking for everyone's next book boyfriend. When it comes to her stories, you can guarantee there will be romance, angst, and, most of all, there will be love that lasts a lifetime.

CONNECT WITH REBECCA

Website - www.rebeccahchase.com

Twitter - twitter.com/rebeccahchase

Facebook - www.facebook.com/RebeccaHChaseAuthor

Tiktok - @rebeccachaseauthor

Instagram and Threads – rebeccahchase

Goodreads - 15019280.Rebecca_Chase

Printed in Great Britain
by Amazon

38247032R00148